ROMANCING LADY AUGUSTA

The Welwyn Marriage Wager
Book 4

By

Jenna Jaxon

ARE YOU SIGNED UP FOR DRAGONBLADE'S BLOG?

You'll get the latest news and information on exclusive giveaways, exclusive excerpts, coming releases, sales, free books, cover reveals and more.

Check out our complete list of authors, too!

No spam, no junk. That's a promise!

Sign Up Here

www.dragonbladepublishing.com

Dearest Reader;

Thank you for your support of a small press. At Dragonblade Publishing, we strive to bring you the highest quality Historical Romance from some of the best authors in the business. Without your support, there is no 'us', so we sincerely hope you adore these stories and find some new favorite authors along the way.

Happy Reading!

CEO, Dragonblade Publishing

Additional Dragonblade books by Author Jenna Jaxon

The Welwyn Marriage Wager Series
Until I'm Safe in Your Arms (Book 1)
The Baron's Halo (Book 2)
Yule Be Mine (Book 3)
Romancing Lady Augusta (Book 4)

The Lyon's Den Series
Pride of Lyons
The Lyon's Paw

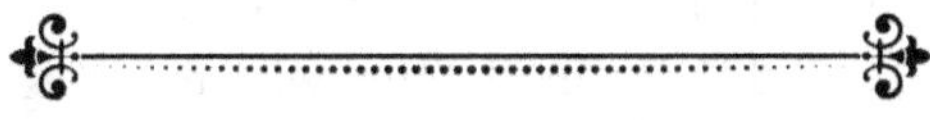

CHAPTER ONE

Tilney Manor
Near Thetford, Norfolk, England
April 1860

"WHEN IS HE supposed to arrive?" Lady Augusta Hardy demanded of her mother, shifting anxiously from one silk-slippered foot to the other as they stood in front of the bay window of the front reception room. Carriage after carriage deposited the myriad guests her parents had invited for a long weekend at their country house just before the beginning of what would be her second Season, but Augusta was interested in only one particular guest.

"Who do you mean, my dear?" Mother waved cheerily at Lady Tolliver, her two very eligible sons now accompanying her up the graveled walkway to the manor's front door. "We have invited a host of young gentlemen for you to meet and become acquainted with this weekend."

"You know very well whom I am speaking of, Mother." Augusta cut a speaking glance to her parent, then instantly turned back to look out to the driveway as another carriage pulled up and disgorged four strapping gentlemen, none of whom Augusta knew in the least.

"Ah, there are the Duke of Welwyn's grandsons." As if ignoring her completely, Mother nodded at the four gentlemen who were laughing and talking amongst themselves very amiably. "They will manage to keep the party lively, I'll be bound." She turned to Augusta and leaned toward her, whispering, "You could do much worse than one of them, my dear. The tallest of them is the duke's heir, Lord Royston, the one with the rugged face is Mr. Quartermain, and the other two are Lord Boxted and his brother, Mr. Price."

Augusta frowned as she perused the quartet of would-be suitors. Lord Royston she dismissed out of hand. She'd not marry a man who would one day become a duke with all that attendant pomp and circumstance. Long ago—at the ripe old age of fifteen—she'd decided that kind of life was not for her. The other three, however, she gave more scrutiny to. The rugged faced one, Mr. Quartermain, had the dashing looks of an outdoors man. That appealed to Augusta and she made a mental note to converse with Mr. Quartermain about what pastimes he was most interested in. The other two she wasn't so sure of. "Which one is Lord Boxted and which is his brother?"

"Lord Boxted has the short, dark, straight hair and the genial smile. His brother is somewhat more slender than him, and has the lighter, curly hair." Her mother's eager voice made Augusta sigh. No doubt she'd be paired with each of these gentlemen at some point in the weekend. "I am certain they will prove delightful companions during the party."

"Mr. Quartermain certainly does take the eye, I will admit." In appearance he was certainly head and shoulders above the others. "Although Lord Boxted has an animated look about him as well." She might as well make her mother happy by assessing the gentlemen her parents had taken some pains to gather for her perusal. But none of these young men could hold a candle to the gentleman for whom she was waiting. "But Mother, you have not answered my question." She turned to her mother, her lips pressed together sternly. "When is Mr. Burton to arrive?"

Her mother looked away guiltily and Augusta's heart sank.

"Please do not tell me you did not invite him. Not after I expressly asked that he be part of the party."

"I did invite him, Augusta. Or I attempted to, despite my misgivings." Her mother looked at her askance. "I truly do not think Mr. Richard Burton would be a proper match for you, my dear."

"But one of these tame gentlemen is?" Why her mother's attitude still angered her, Augusta wasn't quite certain. She'd been having this same conversation with both her parents for the past four years. "Mr. Burton is just as eligible as any of these gentlemen."

"Technically, perhaps, as he comes from a good family, but the man himself is quite as wild as the savages he has lived among all these years." Mother shuddered. "That ghastly scar on his cheek."

"He was still recovering from the injury when we saw him, Mother. He could scarcely be faulted for being wounded whilst escaping from the Somali warriors." Augusta closed her eyes, remembering the dashing explorer who had captured her interest when she was fifteen. Her heart skipped a beat whenever she thought of him. "And I am certain his cheek has healed in the ensuing four years. He will scarcely frighten anyone this weekend."

"I am certain he won't, Augusta, as he will not be here."

"What?" Ever since her parents had told her of this house party—their not-so-subtle bid to have her married before her second Season—she'd been dreaming of spending the entire weekend drinking in the stories from Mr. Burton's own lips.

He'd enthralled her with his tales of the harrowing adventures he'd endured in Somalia during his visit to her father in 1856 and she couldn't wait to hear of his most recent travels first hand. Of course, she'd read every volume he'd written—from *Goa and the Blue Mountains* to the recently published *Lake Regions of Central Equatorial Africa*—along with as many other travelogues she could convince her father to purchase.

Ever since his visit, the thrill of adventure and the exploration of vast unknown continents had called to Augusta like a siren's song. Oh, if only she could be the wife of such an explorer and go off with him to experience these breathtaking travels for herself. As it was, she'd never even left England and hadn't been any further south than London nor any further north than Carlisle.

However, if she managed to marry the right person, she could perhaps avoid an ordinary life and become an adventurer in her own right, like Sophia Poole or Isabella Bird.

"Why isn't Mr. Burton coming?" The words caught in her throat. This was to have been her chance to talk with him, to show him how much she admired him and his work. To make him understand that she wanted to lead a life of adventure with him.

"According to your father, Mr. Burton declined my invitation as he was scheduled to set sail for America at the beginning of this month." Mother patted Augusta's shoulder. "He proposes to cross the American continent, apparently."

Completely at a loss, Augusta blinked back tears. This wasn't fair. She'd been dreaming of Mr. Burton for so long, had been certain she could take this weekend to persuade him she would be a good wife and companion on his explorations, that now she didn't know what she was going to do. All the other gentlemen of her acquaintance paled in her estimation beside what the dashing Mr. Burton had done. How could she settle for one of them?

"Besides, Augusta, you must have known Mr. Burton has been engaged to marry Miss Arundell for years now." Her mother's face held a jot of sympathy.

"But they are not married yet."

"Because her family also disapproves of Mr. Burton."

And thank God for that. As long as he wasn't married, there was still hope for Augusta yet. "I cannot see how anyone would disapprove of such a heroic gentleman. He has faced more trials and tribulations in his efforts to gather knowledge of the world than anyone else alive, Mother. I don't see how anyone could find fault with his character."

"My dear, you are taken in by the glamourous reports of Mr. Burton's exploits. But I highly doubt you would find day-to-day life with the man quite so romantic." Her mother shuddered. "You would seriously think of living for months on end in a tent with strange gentlemen and native servants? Eating God knows what, in climates so hot and humid they would try the patience of a saint?"

"I would find anything preferable to the inane social conversations and wretched weather of England, Mother." How could she contemplate life as her mother had known it all these years with nothing but the unending rounds of social seasons and the dreary cold, dampness that plagued all of England most of the time. Augusta tugged her silk shawl closer around her shoulders and cast a glance up at the darkening sky. Rain before nightfall, no doubt. The thought of cloudless skies and hot winds was idyllic to Augusta.

"In any case, Mr. Burton will not be in attendance this weekend, so I beg of you, Augusta, converse with the young gentlemen we have invited. Dance with them." Mother's voice had taken on a commanding tone. "You may even find one of them amusing enough to rival Mr. Burton. I am sure most of them have enjoyed a Grand Tour or have had interesting travels, if that's what interests you most." Her mother turned toward the door. "Come, let me introduce these young men to you."

Instead Augusta returned her gaze to the driveway where two more gentlemen were embarking from their carriages, umbrellas held over their heads even though there would be no rain for hours. Mr. Burton, she'd venture to guess, didn't even own an umbrella. He was an adventurer who took the weather as it came in the worst possible places and likely didn't even notice. He'd scoff at these dandies who needed to stay dry at any cost. She'd scoff at them as well.

Her parents could parade every eligible *parti* in front of her this weekend and it wouldn't make a bit of difference. She'd wait for Mr. Burton to return from America and find a way to meet with him. He'd been engaged to Miss Arundell for years and nothing had come of it. But, if she could manage to get Mr. Burton alone for ten minutes, she'd find a way to change his mind about whom he wished to marry.

"YOU'VE LOST THAT wager before it's begun, Harry." Julius Price, Lord Boxted, laughed and plucked the family's book of wagers from his breast coat pocket where it always resided and thumbed toward the middle of the small leather volume. He fished a pencil out of the same pocket and wrote down the bet in his precise handwriting. "Harry wagers he will be the first of the four of us to dance with Lady Augusta Hardy. Who's going to take that on?" He glanced at the three faces grinning back at him. They'd spent the entire train ride from London devising wagers of different sorts. Now it seemed as though the short carriage ride from the station to the Tilney's manor house wouldn't be any different.

"Fifty pounds says he does." His cousin Ulysses Quartermain stretched out his long legs and sent a disgusted glance at Harry. "I'll even wager a further fifty that Lady Tilney has already arranged for Harry to lead Lady Augusta out first. Who wouldn't wish her daughter to marry the heir to a dukedom?"

"I'm with Yule." Francis piped up. "Put me down for twenty on Harry."

"My own brother wagers against me." Julius shook his head, but grinned as he dutifully wrote it down. "I will then be the only one wagering against Harry. I'll take both your fifties and your twenty, Francis and say that I will be the first to dance with Lady Augusta. No matter what her mother may say, I have a feeling about the lady."

"Oh, a feeling is it, brother?" Francis dug his elbow into Julius' s side as the carriage pulled up before the front of the gray stone manor house. "Have you met Lady Augusta before?"

"No, but our mother knows Lady Tilney quite well, and I managed to find out quite a bit about her." Julius's smile deepened. "Knowledge I hope to use to impress the lady and therefore secure the first dance this weekend."

"I'm not certain knowledge of the lady's habits or likes and dislikes will trump a dukedom, but I stand by my wager." The carriage door opened and Harry clambered out.

"So do I, cousin." Julius followed directly after him, leaving Francis and Yule to emerge on their own. Julius took in the stately gray stone building, a front portico framed by white marble columns leading into the manor house.

Windows graced either side of the portico, the left one revealing two ladies peering out at the arriving guests. The older lady, possibly Lady Tilney, was smiling at him and his companions. The younger lady, however, was peering up at the gathering clouds overhead, a disgruntled look on her face. It was an interesting face despite its annoyed look. Eyes set wide apart in an oval-shaped face, with thick dark brows above gave her a look of intelligence. Her pale green gown, what he could see of it, became her complexion, and her ebony hair was curled and pulled back with flowers adorning it here and there. She'd be quite lovely if she smiled.

As Julius continued to assess the lady, she kept her eyes on the weather, her expression not changing. Perhaps Lady Augusta—and if the other one was Lady Tilney this must certainly be her daughter—disliked the prospect of being cooped up by a rainstorm in the house with all her prospective suitors. If the weather cleared tomorrow, he'd suggest a stroll with her in the garden or perhaps an early morning ride. His mother had said Lady Augusta was fond of riding and Julius meant to make the most of that information. Not that Lady Augusta was the lady he meant to court, but he did wish to win the wager with his cousins. The better she knew him, the more inclined she might be to grant him the first dance.

Turning his attention to the others, Julius headed into the foyer, where the two ladies stood to welcome them. "Good afternoon, Lady Tilney. Thank you so much for inviting us for the weekend."

"You are most welcome, Lord Boxted." Lady Tilney curtseyed to the four of them. "Gentlemen. My dear," she turned to the young lady beside her, "may I introduce Lord Boxted, Lord Royston, Mr. Price, and Mr. Quartermain. Gentlemen, this is my daughter, Lady Augusta."

Lady Augusta dropped a curtsey. "I am honored to meet you, gentlemen." She raised a piercing blue gaze to them. "I do hope you enjoy yourselves this weekend."

"I am certain we will, Lady Augusta." Harry stepped forward, all smiles. "With such a lovely companion, how could we not?"

The lady's lips puckered, as though she wasn't sure if she wished to smile or send Harry a stern set-down. "I suppose that remains to be seen, Lord Royston." Her unfaltering gaze took in each of them, as though they were stallions at Tattersall's and she wanted to make the best use of her money. "I look forward to furthering our acquaintance during the party."

"Hawkins will see you to your rooms." Lady Tilney nodded to the butler who was taking care of the newest arrivals, then looped her arm through Lady Augusta's. "Come my dear. Let me introduce you to Lady Camford's sons." They moved past Julius toward a party of three who had just entered the foyer.

With a sigh, Julius presented himself to Hawkins who instructed a footman to show him and his cousins to their rooms. As it was early afternoon, once he and his companions had changed, they would need to amuse themselves until the gong was rung for dinner, some hours away.

"I say, should we settle in a bit, then meet downstairs for billiards?" Julius suggested as they followed the footman up the staircase to the first floor.

"Fine by me." Francis ducked into the chamber the footman indicated to him.

"Give me half an hour to change and I'll meet you at the bottom of the main staircase." Harry stuck his head out of his door, then with a quick nod to them, turned and shut the door.

Nodding absently, Julius entered his room, noting the room's appointments were more than adequate and signaled his valet to begin the transformation from dusty traveling clothes to an informal suit of navy wool. After a splash of cologne water, Julius headed out and down the stairs where he found Yule and Francis waiting for him. "Is Harry lollygagging again?"

"Nothing new there," Yule drawled. "Shall we press on and find the billiards before someone else beats us to it?"

"Agreed. Francis, will you wait for Harry?" Julius had already snagged a passing footman. "The billiard room?"

"Just there, my lord." The servant pointed down the corridor toward the back of the manor house. "The last door on the right across from the study."

"Thank you." Julius turned toward the hallway indicated. "Come down as soon as Harry arrives." He and Yule hurried along the corridor until they turned into the billiards room, only to find it already occupied by a lively game already in progress. "Bollocks." Julius gave Yule a weary look. "Let's check out the study. Hopefully Lord Tilney is well stocked with libations."

They stepped across the corridor to find the study devoid of people, but well stocked with both a cut crystal decanter of spirits and glasses and a chess set. Julius sent a glance to Yule. "You pour the drinks and I'll set up the board."

By the time Harry and Francis had found their way in, Julius was six moves into the game and Yule, having already lost two pawns, a rook, both knights, and a bishop, was scowling like a gargoyle.

"You should know better, Yule." Francis helped himself to a drink. "Jules can win at chess in his sleep. I've given up hope of ever beating him. I now wager on how long I can hold out before checkmate."

"He is not that good." Harry had come to stand over Julius's shoulder, which bothered Julius not at all. From a young age, chess had been his favorite game. The strategic moves played themselves out in his head effortlessly until, as Francis said, he found it difficult to find anyone who could best him.

"And checkmate, Yule." Julius moved his queen into position, pinning Yule's king without a way out.

"Was that eight moves?" Yule looked up, shaking his head.

"Yes." Julius leaned back and sipped his drink, smiling. Not that his cousin had been challenging, but it was good to play new opponents. "Are you up for a game, Harry?"

"Of course." Harry sat down in the seat Yule quickly vacated behind the white ivory pieces and began resetting them. "Shall we wager?"

"On the outcome?" Julius raised an eyebrow. He didn't wish to seem cocky and granted, he hadn't played chess with Harry in years. Still, he'd not been beaten at chess in a good six months and that had been at his club by Lord Steadman, who was admittedly a world-class player.

Harry glanced at Francis who shook his head emphatically. "Well, no." He sighed. "On the number of moves until checkmate."

"Agreed." Julius grabbed the betting book. "How many moves, then?"

Harry looked at Yule, then back to the board. "Ten."

"Done." Julius laid the book on the table beside him. "Your move."

Seven moves later, Julius had taken Harry's queen, two bishops, a rook and a knight. "I believe that is checkmate, cuz."

"How do you do that?" Harry stood up, bewildered. He headed for the decanter to refill his glass.

"I'm never exactly sure how." Julius began to put the pieces back on the board. "I see the moves in my head, sometimes six or seven ahead. I don't know how else to explain it."

"I do the same thing, my lord."

Julius's head snapped toward the study door that had opened

silently, allowing Lady Augusta to enter the room without warning.

"You might have ended it in six if you'd moved the knight to king's four one move earlier." Apparently, she'd been standing there for some time.

Staring at her and rising slowly, Julius nodded. "I thought I'd give my cousin an extra move. He'd wagered he'd go ten, but I knew he wouldn't last that long."

A smile touched her lips, making her face suddenly quite beautiful. "Generous in victory, although not too generous." The lady moved further into the room, coming to stand in front of Julius. "If I wager I can take you in ten moves, will you allow me to play, Lord Boxted?"

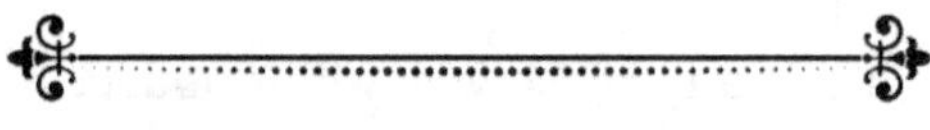

CHAPTER TWO

STARTLED BY THE lady's request, Julius stared first at her, then shot a glance over to the others hoping to gauge their reactions, only to be met with foolish grins. "You play chess, my lady?"

"From time to time." Her smile continued, although it seemed to be masking some other emotion as well. Humor, perhaps? She moved to the small table where the chessboard sat and began resetting the pieces. "My father taught me to play when I was quite young."

Though it was not unheard of for ladies to play chess—his own mother had been known to play occasionally with his father—Julius still was startled at the notion of playing against Lady Augusta. Another glance at his cousins and brother showed their faces filled with mirth at the idea that the lady proposed not to simply play him in chess but actually to beat him. If it didn't seem rude to refuse, Julian would have declined the offer. However, the lady had declared her wish for a wager, and that he could not refuse.

"Then I shall be happy to accept your wager and play with you." He moved back to the table and indicated the chair opposite him. "Please be seated."

She finished setting up the chessboard, then sat in the chair Harry had vacated. Julius took his seat and looked at her expectantly.

"What do you wish to wager, my lord?"

"The first dance at tomorrow night's ball, my lady." The notion of that bet had occurred to him as soon as the lady had mentioned the word "wager."

A chorus of groans arose from his audience, Harry's voice being the loudest.

Lady Augusta peered at them briefly then returned her attention back to the board. "That is if you win or I take longer than ten moves to win." She looked up, that puckered smile back in place. "I think if I best you in less than ten moves, I should not pay a forfeit."

"Of course not, my lady." The idea that she would win in less than ten moves was rather charming.

"And what will you forfeit in the event you lose, my lord?" Her intense blue eyes were on him, and suddenly Julius found himself swallowing hard.

"Um…" He couldn't look away from her penetrating azure gaze. "I lose the first dance with you?"

"Perhaps you should lose all chance of partnering me tomorrow evening." Her even tone coupled with the power of her regard unnerved Julius to no end.

But he nodded just the same. "I will accept that wager, Lady Augusta." Now he certainly had an incentive to win, as if he'd needed one. "Will you begin the play?"

Lady Augusta nodded, then without hesitation moved her pawn. "King's pawn to king four."

"King's pawn to king four." Julius countered, interested to see her next move. It would tell him so much about her level of skill.

"King's bishop's pawn to king's bishop four."

Julius stared at the board. Was the lady going for the King's Gambit opening? Or simply moving the pieces? Time to find out. "Pawn takes pawn."

"King's knight to king's bishop three." She moved the piece so quickly it seemed to fly.

That settled one thing. This was definitely the King's Gambit opening. And Lady Augusta was apparently very familiar with it. Julius pulled his tumultuous thoughts back to the board and considered his options. "King's knight's pawn to king's knight four."

"Queen's knight to queen's bishop three." Lady Augusta moved the knight then sat back, gazing at him evenly.

What a random move on her part. She'd started out well, but that move had left her vulnerable on several fronts. "Pawn to king's knight four." He smiled and began to think of a popular waltz tune in his head. Perhaps he could make certain the orchestra played a waltz for the first dance tomorrow night.

She moved her knight and he countered by bringing his queen into play threatening her king.

Holding Lady Augusta closely in his arms would be oh so satisfying. She really was quite a stunning wo—

"Queen to king's knight four."

The tune in his head halted abruptly as the board came into focus and Julius stared uncomprehending at the white queen that now threatened his queen. He shot a surreptitious glance at his opponent, whose face stared serenely back at him.

This lady was a worthy opponent indeed. But he could recover. "Pawn to king's knight seven." She would obviously then take his queen but he would get it back when his pawn took her rook and he would threaten her bishop and king.

Two moves later her queen's knight took his bishop's pawn and Lady Augusta sat back, a smile on her lips once more as she announced, "Checkmate."

A stunned silence emanated from his brother and cousins.

In shock, Julius stared at the board and immediately realized his error. Almost all his pieces remained in the first two ranks of his side of the board. He'd neglected to develop his attack because he'd been too busy trying to decide if Lady Augusta understood the tactics of the game to worry about his own strategy. Neither had it helped that he'd allowed himself to become distracted by the thought of enjoying his spoils rather than actually winning them. He'd underestimated his opponent grossly, something he'd not done since his earliest days learning the game. There was nothing left to do save take his defeat like a gentleman.

"Indeed it is, my lady." He met her amused gaze with a rueful smile. "Congratulations on a well-played game."

"Thank you, my lord." She rose, bringing him to his feet. "Perhaps we can play again sometime this weekend."

"I will look forward to a rematch, Lady Augusta." At least next time he would know his opponent's strengths and try to guard against his own weaknesses. And he'd get to spend some more time with her.

"Allow me to congratulate you, Lady Augusta." Harry had stepped forward, breaking the silence of his equally stunned audience. "And as your first dance now is quite free, I'd like to request the honor of it at tomorrow night's ball."

Leave it to Harry to swoop in and take advantage not only of Julius's humiliating defeat, but secure their earlier wager as well.

Lady Augusta sent Julius a sympathetic glance but nodded to his cousin. "As I have not promised it elsewhere, my lord, I will be happy to grant it to you."

Harry's look of triumph galled Julius to no end, but he couldn't fault his cousin for taking advantage of the situation. He'd have done the same thing had their positions been reversed.

"Might I have the second dance then, Lady Augusta?" Yule stepped closer, a twinkle in his eye. "I wouldn't want you to be in danger of becoming a wallflower."

"Neither would I, my lady." Francis eagerly came up on the lady's other side. "May I solicit the third dance of the evening?" He looked pointedly at Julius. "I'm afraid you will need to seek other partners after that, although I for one will be happy to partner you any time during the evening."

"I applaud your enthusiasm, Mr. Price," Lady Augusta looked around the small circle, from one gentleman to the next, until her gaze finally rested on Julius. "But I fear I must spread my favors in a wide circle to include the many gentlemen here this weekend." Her intense blue eyes captured Julius once more. "Although unfortunately not all of them."

There were snorts of suppressed laughter from his companions.

"But if you will excuse me gentlemen, I must find my mother and see if anyone else has arrived." She curtsied and turned to the door, her hooped skirts gracefully tilting as she left the room.

Julius turned a glowering frown on his cousins, then deepened it as he took in his brother's grinning face. "Et tu, Brute?"

"All's fair in love and war, Jules," Francis chuckled. "I suppose this could be considered both."

"You all certainly lost no time looting and pillaging Lady Augusta's dance card." Julius fought hard to keep the bitterness out of his voice. He had no one but himself to blame for being excluded from dancing with the lady.

"To the victor go the spoils, old chap." Harry beamed at him. "You can wait until we return to London to settle our earlier wager." He gave Julius an innocent look. "Who knows but that you may lose more wagers before the end of the weekend."

"I'd nobble you Harry, if you weren't grandfather's heir." Julius glowered at him, and sighed deeply. So much for his plans to charm Lady Augusta.

"The billiard room is free now. Let's go before someone else nips in." Yule was already halfway out the room.

Harry downed his brandy and followed suit.

"You coming, Jules?" Francis paused at the doorway.

"In a minute. I want to reset the board." He kept his eyes on the chess pieces as he set them one by one on the black and white squares. More black pieces to be righted than white unfortunately.

"Sure." Francis lingered however—Julius could feel his twin hesitating in the doorway. "You won't be long?"

"Not at all." Julius righted his king. *Hubris, thy name is Julius.*

His brother left and Julius sat back in his seat, the white

queen clasped in his hand. Lady Augusta had been a worthy foe and he'd gotten what he deserved for underestimating her. He'd not do that again this weekend. And as he was banished from her dance card, he'd have to devise other ways to become better acquainted with the lady. Not only did she possess the dark beauty he was always attracted to, but she clearly had an exemplary mind with pinpoint focus. These points of her character intrigued him to a degree he'd never felt before.

Odd that he'd had no idea of actually looking for a wife this weekend. When he and Francis and their cousins had received the invitation, it had been more of a lark for the four of them. A way to get in some early hunting before the heat of the summer drove all thoughts of shooting or stalking out of their minds until the Glorious Twelfth.

Now however, Lady Augusta had piqued his interest. So it would become his mission this weekend to get to know her better, develop the Lady Augusta Gambit to assure that he gained back the advantage as quickly as he could.

AUGUSTA HURRIED DOWN the corridor, back toward the foyer, ostensibly looking for her mother, but actually hoping to find her father. More than anything, she wanted to tell him about her match with Lord Boxted, to garner his praise for besting a very worthy opponent. The whole episode had left her quite giddy.

"There you are, my dear." Her mother scurried out of the large receiving room, now crowded with more arriving guests. "Come with me a moment. I must introduce Lords Bude and Bideford to you."

With a sigh, Augusta followed her mother into the receiving room and was duly introduced to two more young gentlemen she would likely dance and converse with this weekend and then never see again. Once they had taken their leave, she leaned toward her mother and whispered, "How many eligible gentlemen have you invited for the weekend?"

"Twenty-six."

Augusta gasped, appalled that she would have to be obliging to so many young men over the course of the next four days.

"However, only eighteen accepted the invitation." her mother continued, and Augusta gave up a prayer of thanksgiving. "Lords Winkleigh and Silverton were otherwise engaged, Lord Tadley was taken ill at the last minute, poor man, Sir Joshua Noonan's uncle died last week and he's in mourning, Mr. Simon Farquar and his brother, Mr. John Farquar are now betrothed to Miss Mary Simmons and her sister, Miss Grace Simmons." Her mother paused and pursed her lips. "I do so dislike when brothers marry a set of sisters. It strikes me as being in bad taste for some reason."

"I am certain that is your own prejudice, Mother, and not a usual censure of Society." Scarcely paying attention, Augusta glanced around, still looking for her father.

"Mr. Coleman's mother is ill and he must attend to her. And of course, Mr. Burton is out of the country."

That brought Augusta's attention back to her parent and the daunting idea that she would be almost the sole focus of eighteen gentlemen's devotion for the next few days. She'd have preferred to meet them in smaller groups or not at all if Mr. Burton was not among their number, although she must say, she'd enjoyed her encounter with the Duke of Welwyn's four grandsons. Hopefully, if she simply must engage with the rest of the gentlemen, they would make as good an impression on her as those four had.

At last she spied her father. "Mother, I must go speak with Father. A matter of some importance."

"What kind of—"

Before her mother could detain her, Augusta hurried into the foyer and joined the circle of gentlemen that included her father. "Good afternoon, gentlemen."

They all murmured "good day" and bowed. Before they all

turned their gaze on her and attempted to begin a conversation, she smiled at them all, but took her father's arm. "Father, I wonder if I could have a word with you. Something rather extraordinary has happened."

Her father's eyebrows rose, but he nodded. "Gentlemen, if you will excuse us."

Augusta grasped his arm and steered him toward the only quiet spot she could think of, the formal dining room. The servants had already begun laying the table, but their presence was of no matter. She drew her father into one of the room's corners, and smiled up at him. "Father, you will never guess what just occurred."

"Have you received a proposal already, Augusta?" His eyes were filled with mirth. "I admit, I did scoff when your mother told that was the purpose of this house party, but if her scheme has worked this quickly, I fear I will have to apologize to her forthwith."

"Truly, Father, this is no time for your questionable sense of humor." She shifted impatiently from one foot to the other. "No, there has been no proposal and as Mr. Burton is not to be among the guests this weekend, I can tell you I do not expect to receive, nor do I intend to accept any proposal offered me."

"Then what, pray tell, is this extraordinary thing that has happened?" Her father crossed his arms over his chest but seemed ready to listen to her.

"I had wandered down the corridor to see who was in the billiards room, but when I got to the end of the hall, there was animated conversation coming from the study. I stepped in there and found the Duke of Welwyn's four grandsons holding a series of chess matches." Augusta was almost breathless by the time she'd set the scene for him. "Lord Boxted had apparently beaten all of his cousins by the time I arrived and I asked if he would allow me to play."

"From the look on your face, my dear, I assume he was amenable to that request." Father's lips puckered in a smile.

"He was." Augusta sighed with satisfaction just thinking of the moment.

"Did you use the King's Gambit?"

"I did." Her grin spread as wide as possible across her face.

"How many moves did it take for you to win?" Her father's tone said it was a foregone conclusion, which made her fill with pride.

"Eight."

"Excellent, my dear. Well done." The glowing praise meant more to Augusta than the actual victory had. Her father cocked his head. "How did Lord Boxted take the loss?"

"In a most gentleman-like manner, Father. I'm certain it hurt his vanity to be bested by anyone, much less a lady. But he congratulated me warmly." Augusta remembered the steady look in his dark blue eyes. "And is prepared to abide by the wager he lost."

"What did you wager?" Her father's eyes narrowed.

"If he won, he'd have had the first dance at tomorrow evening's ball."

"But as he lost…"

"He will forfeit dancing with me entirely for the evening."

"A rather harsh penalty, I'd say." Father shook his head, but there was approval in his eyes. "I'm certain it will be a thorn in his side all evening."

"I suppose so." Augusta was almost wishing that hadn't been the wager. She'd rather come to like Lord Boxted. A dance with him tomorrow night could have been quite pleasant. "I'm certain we'll partner one another during the Season, though."

"Most likely." Then, as though dismissing the event, he turned to go. "Congratulations on your win, Augusta. I am very proud of my protégée."

"Father." Augusta grasped his arm before he could leave. "Mother told me that Mr. Burton is in America. Do you know when he plans to return?"

Frowning, he turned back to her. "Richard has not made me

privy to that information, Augusta. And I warn you again that the man has never expressed an interest in courting you. Likely because he's been betrothed for years to Miss Arundell." The harsh lines on his face smoothed out and he grasped her hands. "I understand his allure, my dear. You are not the first young lady to become infatuated with him. But I beg of you, seek out the acquaintance of the young men here this weekend and all during the Season. They will serve you better in the long run than losing your heart to Mr. Burton."

"But if Mr. Burton did ask for my hand, you wouldn't refuse him, would you?" Augusta gripped her father's hands, willing him to agree to this much at least. If she could just get that assurance from him, she was certain she could persuade Mr. Burton when the time came.

Father sighed deeply but nodded. "I would not deny his suit, Augusta, however I cannot believe you will manage to get him to propose."

Triumphant for the second time that afternoon, Augusta rose on her tiptoes to kiss her father's cheek. "Never mind about that, Father. All I need is your promise to permit the marriage." She smiled merrily as they headed for the door. "Leave the rest of it to me."

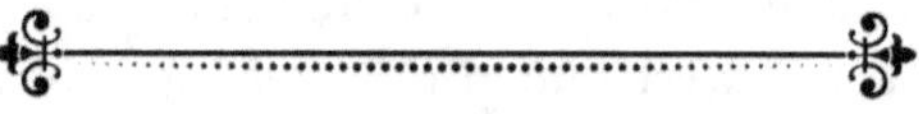

CHAPTER THREE

"ARE YOU FOND of dancing, Lady Augusta?" Lord Royston presented his arm as soon as their dance ended. Smiling breathlessly, Augusta took it. She'd requested a polka to begin the evening's festivities, hoping to take the measure of Lord Royston's abilities on the ballroom floor. Surprisingly, she'd been quite satisfied with his performance.

"I am, my lord. The polka is one of my favorite dances. So spritely and challenging."

"You seem to enjoy challenges, my lady." He chuckled. "My congratulations again on winning at chess yesterday. My cousin is not often bested. You should be exceedingly pleased."

"I have to say I was. He's the first gentleman I've played against other than my father."

"Then your father is to be commended on his very apt pupil." Lord Royston's compliments were gratifying, however she didn't wish to belabor her victory.

"Did you enjoy today's hunt, my lord?" The gentlemen had taken themselves off early in the day to shoot red deer.

"Very much. I had a shot at a buck, but missed by that much." He held up his fingers to show an infinitesimal gap.

"Well, I wish you better luck next time." They had arrived back at the place her mother had taken up as her station for the ball, at the end of the room farthest from the orchestra. Her next partner, Mr. Quartermain, stood next to her, chatting as though they were old friends.

Lord Royston released her arm and bowed crisply. "Thank you so much for the lovely dance, Lady Augusta. If you are not engaged later in the evening, I would like to partner you once more at least."

"You really must give the other chaps a chance, Harry." Lord Boxted appeared like a bolt out of the blue, looking splendid in his well-cut evening dress. "And Lady Augusta must need time to recover from your woefully lacking skills on the dance floor." He smiled as he quipped with his cousin, as though it were of little consequence that he had not won the wager to partner her in the first dance. Then his gaze turned toward her and she caught her breath at the intensity of his countenance. "Good evening, Lady Augusta. I fear I must apologize for losing the wager yesterday."

"A...apologize for losing, my lord?" Something in his penetrating gaze made her shiver—as though he read her mind.

"Yes. You see, if I had won, you would not have been forced to endure my cousin's fumbling attempts at social dancing." His smile electrified her. "Instead, I would have been able to lead you out and show you how a polka should be danced."

Scrambling to pull her thoughts together, Augusta nodded. "That would, of course, have been a fortunate turn of events for me, my lord." She recovered her wits and smiled up at him. "However, I believe I will keep the victory in chess and live for the promise of a future dance with you."

"I will hold you to that promise, Lady Augusta." His blue eyes mesmerized her until a tug on her arm broke her away from Lord Boxted and Mr. Quartermain instead led her onto the dance floor.

Her dance with Mr. Quartermain was a Galop, so there was little time or breath for conversation. The dance was lively, and her partner acquitted himself well, but Augusta's thoughts kept straying back to Lord Boxted. Such a singular gentleman, with a more intense stare than she'd ever encountered before. Well, perhaps save Mr. Burton's dark-eyed gaze. But he'd never peered into her face with the force of Lord Boxted's regard. The gentleman was truly quite thrilling. Such a pity by her own decree she could not dance with him.

The Galop ended and Mr. Quartermain entertained her with a very funny account of the first time he'd ever tried to polka as a lad of ten. They were laughing in earnest by the time they reached her mother where the group of gentlemen milling about her had increased. Lord Boxted was still ready to dance attendance, which spoke well of him. He could have gone off to find a young lady with whom he could dance. Her attention went to Mr. Price, her next partner, standing next to his brother.

"Mr. Price, I believe I am promised to you next if you are not too weary from the hunt today." Augusta gazed at the sea of faces surrounding her and suddenly wished her mother had not been quite so zealous in her efforts to invite half the *ton* for the weekend. She'd like the opportunity to converse more particularly with a few of the guests.

"I must confess, Lady Augusta, I did not avail myself of the hunting today." Mr. Price did not seem abashed at this confession at all. "I do enjoy it, but I kept to the study, writing letters instead. Some correspondence simply cannot wait."

"Did you spend your day writing letters as well, my lord?" Augusta shot a sly glance at Lord Boxted.

"Indeed, I did not." Lord Boxted looked offended that she would have suggested such a thing. "My brother may have demurred in favor of his scribbling, but you will not find me turning down a day of stalking."

"And were you successful today?" She scarcely needed to ask the question, so ebullient was his lordship's demeanor.

"That I was." A wide smile split his handsome face. "I brought down a stag just before lunch. I had a shot at another one later in the afternoon, but the wind shifted and it loped away."

"No need to cull the entire herd single-handedly, Jules," his brother piped up. "You needed to leave some deer for the others to find."

"I assure you, brother, there were plenty to go around." The brothers' sparring was entertaining to watch, but Augusta interrupted them.

"Lord Boxted, are you engaged for the dance after this one?"

"I am not, my lady." Lord Boxted made a small bow. "I have not asked any young lady for a dance this evening. As I am not allowed to dance with you, I intend to spend the time in-between dances amusing you instead."

"Then I am writing your name on my dance card for the next one, which is a mazurka." She took Mr. Price's arm, despite the wide stares of both gentlemen.

"But Lady Augusta—" Lord Boxted's panic was oddly comical. "The wager… I cannot—"

"I have decided to rescind the wager I won and instead require you to dance the mazurka with me." Augusta's thoughts raced as she improvised. "I think that will be a more difficult task than allowing you to laze about all evening not dancing at all." She cocked her head. "You do know the dance, do you not?"

"Yes, my lady." He nodded his head soberly. "I know it quite well."

"Then be prepared when I return with your brother." She tossed her head and steered Mr. Price, who had not a word to say, onto the dance floor. "Cat got your tongue, Mr. Price?"

"Apparently so, my lady." The tall gentleman with the riotously curly hair grinned briefly, then led them off in a waltz. The young man seemed to be concentrating hard on his steps, so Augusta gave him some time to settle into the dance before remarking, "You and your brother seem to be very different, Mr. Price. One would scarcely believe you were brothers at all."

"We are not quite as different as night and day, my lady, but we do not see eye to eye on many things. Lord Boxted quite enjoys the outdoor life of stalking and shooting, riding to the hounds as you may have surmised from his enthusiasm for the hunt today. My tastes run more toward books and music, and the arts in general."

"Then you do not hunt or ride?" Augusta had never met a gentleman who didn't enjoy those sorts of pastimes.

"Oh, I can and I do from time to time, usually to keep my brother or cousins company, but I don't enjoy it nearly as much as they do." He met her startled gaze and his eyes crinkled as he smiled. "What we are all most passionate about, however, is wagering. You may have heard us in the study yesterday for we were so engrossed in the wagering and the game, none of us realized you had entered the room until you spoke."

"You all did seem consumed with your wager. Your brother seemed terribly outraged just now when I changed the rules." Augusta had been startled at the vehemence in Lord Boxted's voice when he tried to keep to the terms of the original wager.

"My entire family, the Quartermain side of it at least, is like that. Nothing is so sacred to any of us as making wagers and fulfilling the terms of them." Mr. Price shook his head as they rounded the turn at the end of the dance floor. "Wagers are usually considered debts of honor, my lady. However, my family takes that axiom to heart to a serious degree. Nothing could ever induce any of us to renege on a wager."

"Well, I hope Lord Boxted was not offended that I merely changed the forfeit."

"Oh, I daresay he was not. Startled perhaps, but not offended." The gentleman who held her in his arms tilted his head to the side, like a curious bird. "Why *did* you decide to do that, my lady?"

Now it was Augusta's turn to disguise her intentions. "As I said, it seemed a much more difficult task for Lord Boxted to dance the mazurka with me than to stand idly about all evening."

"You think that, do you, my lady?" Mr. Price's mouth puckered, trying not to smile. "Well, I will leave you to be the judge of that after your dance." He twirled her one more time, then they bowed to one another, and he offered his arm. "Thank you very much for the waltz. It is my favorite of the dances."

"Thank you, Mr. Price." Augusta kept her face shielded from his by nodding to several people as they made their way back to her mother. "It was rather illuminating."

Mr. Price gave her over to her mother and the crowd of gentlemen closed in on her, those whom she had not granted dances to yet putting themselves forward most forcefully.

"Now gentlemen, I am certain dances can be found for all or most of you." Augusta removed her dance card and pencil from her reticule and studied the remaining slots. There were fewer than she'd thought. "Mr. Eastman I can give you the third polka. Sir Roger, will you take the dance directly after supper?" She wrote busily, all too aware of Lord Boxted hovering at her elbow. "Lord Boxted you are down for the mazurka that's making up now."

"Thank you, my lady. I feared you might have changed your mind—again."

She darted a glance at him to find his gaze intent upon her. Augusta's hand clenched her pencil, but she hadn't thought about her silk gloves. The pencil shot out of her fingers and Lord Boxted nimbly caught it before it hit the floor.

"I believe this is yours, my lady." He tried to hold his countenance, but his mouth quivered with scarcely contained mirth.

"Thank you." She would not smile at the smug wretch, although those around him were chuckling and making comments about his agility. Why did the man fascinate and unnerve her by turns?

"We should start toward the dance floor, Lady Augusta. We don't want to be tardy, now do we?" He offered his arm.

Augusta glanced around at the gentlemen still asking for dances and threw up her hands. "I will complete my dance card after this next dance, gentlemen. There are several slots still free, never fear." Hastily, she stowed the card and pencil back in her reticule and took Lord Boxted's arm. "Ready, my lord."

They hurried to the dance floor where couples were gathering into groups of four. Augusta and Lord Boxted took their places in the group nearest to the orchestra. Excited as always when about to dance this most demanding dance, Augusta stood, going over the intricate steps in her head. She'd danced this a hundred times, but she didn't wish to miss any steps while dancing with Lord Boxted.

As though aware of her trepidations, her partner leaned over and whispered, "You have no cause for alarm, my lady. Rely on me and enjoy the dance."

Stunned, Augusta jerked her gaze up to him, but the music began and they bowed to one another, then to their corner couples, and they were off, circling left, leaping in the spritely steps of the mazurka. Almost immediately, Augusta realized her partner had spoken nothing but the truth. Despite the intricate steps of the dance, Lord Boxted danced as though he'd been born to do it. He anticipated every movement and in turn, led Augusta with such sure steps she need never even think about what to do next.

This was an unexpected boon. She'd chosen this dance to see if Lord Boxted was indeed made of sterner stuff than even she had thought. She scarcely needed to think at all as they turned and twirled around the ballroom. Like gliding on air, without a care in the world.

Never had Augusta danced with such a skillful partner. If the dance hadn't been so strenuous, she might have tried to talk with the gentleman, but even she needed to conserve her breath during such a quick moving dance, excellent partner or not. She could, however, smile at him, and did so with pleasure. Lord Boxted seemed a gentleman who did a great many things and did them well. Very much like Mr. Richard Burton. It might not be the worst idea to continue to discover if Lord Boxted had other parts of his character that were similar to Mr. Burton's. With that gentleman out of England for the foreseeable future, it would do her no harm to consider other suitors as well.

Almost before she knew it, the mazurka was at an end. Augusta curtsied to her partner, breathing quite heavily. Lord

Boxted, on the other hand, appeared completely unaffected by the strenuous pace of the dance. He bowed and offered his arm. With a nod, Augusta took it, then snapped open her fan to cool her face.

"Thank you, Lady Augusta, for that lovely dance."

"My thanks to you as well, my lord. That was quite the most fun I've had on the dance floor tonight." Pity she wouldn't have the pleasure of a second dance with him, but the other gentlemen would be slighted if she favored him with another.

"Please accept my heartfelt gratitude for allowing me to dance with you, my lady. By rights I should have been relegated merely to watching you dance from afar this evening." He squeezed her arm. "I must thank you again for allowing me the honor and pure pleasure of partnering you instead."

"You are most welcome, my lord. It was well worth changing the wager." Well worth it.

"Now for the remainder of the evening, I shall have to devise some wagers with the gentlemen to whom you have promised the rest of your dances."

"Why would you do that?" Too quickly they had arrived back at her mother.

"If I can persuade them to wager their dances with you, then I have a better than even chance of partnering you once more, Lady Augusta." He bowed and kissed the air above her hand as he relinquished her to her parent. "The thought of such a possibility will keep me well occupied for the rest of this evening."

With a flourish, he turned and headed toward a little knot of gentlemen on the fringes of the ballroom.

Augusta watched his progress until her next partner came forward to claim her for a polka and she reluctantly turned her attention to him. Thoughts of Lord Boxted—of his grace and skill on the dance floor as well as his handsome visage and tall frame— kept intruding on her time with Mr. Easton, a decent enough dancer if one had not just danced with the sublime.

When the Season began in earnest, she must really think

seriously about Lord Boxted. If any gentleman of the *ton* could hold a candle to Mr. Burton, she'd wager a year's clothing allowance Lord Boxted was the one.

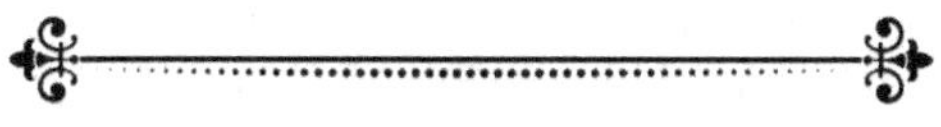

CHAPTER FOUR

London
August 22, 1860

JULIUS WALKED OUT of his grandfather's townhouse, thrilled and horrified by turns. His grandfather had just fired a cannonball that landed in the midst of him, his brother, and four of their closest cousins. A wager—well that was no great surprise, not in the Quartermain family. The horrible surprise, however had been Grandfather's claim that he was dying, prompting his astonishing wager among the six of them: if they could all marry within the next year, each of them would receive an estate, a carriage with equipage, and ten thousand pounds. It was an offer that none of them, in the end, were willing to refuse.

"Jules! Wait up."

He turned back to find Francis almost running after him.

"You were always a fast walker when you were off thinking about something." His brother was puffing as he caught up to him.

"Grandfather gave us a hell of a lot to think about." Julius shook his head. The wager was fantastical, even to him with his title and generous allowance.

"That he did." Francis fell into step beside him. "So, do you think it's really true? That Grandfather is dying?"

Julius jerked his head toward his twin. "I just had the same thought. What if he's cooked up this excuse just to lend credence to the wager? All of us wouldn't have agreed to such a thing if it weren't to please a dying man."

"Or obtain a hefty prize." Francis's eyes gleamed in the afternoon sun. "You're the heir, with a title already and an assured inheritance. To most of the rest of us, Jules, it's a godsend."

"It's a godsend to me as well, Francis." When his brother frowned quizzically, Julius thumped him on the shoulder. "It's a sign that I should go ahead and ask for Lady Augusta's hand in marriage."

"I'm surprised you haven't done so before now." The quizzical look on his brother's face took Julius by surprise. "Why haven't you? I saw you together quite a lot during the Season. I think Mother and Father expected an announcement before now."

"I might have done, especially at the end of the Season. As you say, we'd seen each other at almost every entertainment, dancing, playing cards." He looked slyly at Francis. "Playing chess."

"I take it you let her beat you again?" Francis sniggered. It was the family's favorite joke now.

"I've told you and everyone else, I did not allow Lady Augusta to win that first game. I was distracted by her and simply didn't pay attention to what she was doing." It was a point of honor with Julius that he make it clear the lady had won on her own merits. Of course, no one wanted to listen to that.

"And so you have won your subsequent games with her?"

"No." Julius huffed out his breath. "They have all been draws."

"All of them?" Now the skeptical tone of his brother's voice was reinforced by the upward quirk of his eyebrow.

"There were only two games and no, I did not plan that. The lady is an excellent player. I don't know why everyone in the family finds that difficult to believe." Even when he concentrated on the board, Lady Augusta always seemed to think two moves ahead of him. He'd been damned lucky their third game had been a draw.

"I will take your word for it, brother." Francis gave a final smirk. "In any case, we digress from the question at hand, which is why you have not proposed yet. But can we slow down a bit." Francis was beginning to puff. "You're going to wind me."

Dutifully, Julius slowed his pace. "I was actually on the verge of a declaration in June, but something I overheard her say to her friend, Miss Washer, made me pause."

"Miss Washer is the young lady Lady Tilney sponsored this Season, isn't she?"

"Yes, and she and Lady Augusta became thick as thieves during the summer. We were at Mrs. Pomfrey's garden party and I was coming back with cups of lemonade for the ladies. As I approached them, I heard Lady Augusta say that someone was out of the country, and that is why she wasn't already betrothed." That had given Julius a nasty shock to say the least.

He'd thought from their spirited conversations and general enjoyment of each other's company that the lady had as much affection for him as he had for her. He'd planned to see her father and make his declaration when the *ton*'s festivities were over but before the Tilneys set off for their primary seat in Norfolk. But Lady Augusta's words had held him back for fear of a refusal. He'd tried to find out whom she might expect a proposal from, but none of his family could tell him a thing, and it wasn't something he could just ask anyone. Certainly not the people who would know, such as Lord Tilney, or Miss Washer or of course, Lady Augusta herself.

"But now you've changed your mind?" Francis's question brought him back from his ruminations.

"Well, yes, I have." They turned up the walk to their parents' townhouse. The rest of the family had gone to the country, but the house had been opened up for them when their grandfather had summoned them to London. "At least, today's turn of events has made me think I should at least confer with Lord Tilney. If I ask for her hand and he says she's already spoken for, then I'm no worse off, really. At least I will definitely know where I stand."

"True. And if she's not pre-contracted, then you can certainly make an effort to sweep her off her feet." Francis grinned as the butler took their hats.

They continued to the library, their preferred place to sit, talk, and drink when they were in the townhouse.

"Exactly." Julius poured each of them two fingers worth of brandy and handed a glass to his brother. He sipped his spirits, wondering what exactly he could do to persuade Lady Augusta that he was the preferable choice for a husband. The task would be less daunting if only he knew who his competition was.

"Well, I wish you luck, old chap. I think you and the lady suit admirably." Francis chuckled as he sank into one of the comfortable brown leather chairs. "As long as you stay away from the chessboard."

"But that's where you're wrong, dear brother." Julius too sat in one of the soft leather seats. "We are never better together than when we are competing, or showing off our talents to the other. I always want to do my best to impress Lady Augusta, and I believe she does the same with me. Even when we are just conversing, the urge to banter with one another takes over and suddenly we have to outdo one another in a battle of words." Julius shivered, remembering the last time they had traded quips. It had been of so satisfying and not a little arousing.

"Sounds exhausting if you ask me, old chap." Francis sipped his drink then leaned his head back against the cushion. "Beautiful and vivacious I can take, however a little of the latter goes a long way with me. I prefer a lady with soft edges, a good sense of humor, and the intelligence to appreciate and laugh at my jokes, even when they are not particularly funny."

"And is this paragon of virtue a plain-faced lady as well? Do her sterling qualities more than make up for her lack of beauty?" Julius shot his brother a sardonic glance.

"Not at all." Francis got a far-away look in his eyes. "She is the most beautiful, most enchanting creature you could imagine, Jules."

"Do you mean to tell me you've found such a lady already and didn't care to tell your family, your *twin*, about her?" Julius sat up, suddenly alert. "All right, brother. Spill the beans."

Francis shook his head violently. "I can't."

"Why not?" A sickening thought shot through Julius. "She's not married, is she?"

"God, no." Francis sat up and ran his hand through his hair as though he'd like to pull it out by the roots. "It's not that." He sighed deeply. "I'm having trouble convincing her to marry me."

"What is her objection? It cannot be your breeding or family connections." Even without a title, Francis was a very eligible *parti*.

"No, but she has other concerns…that I cannot speak of, Jules. I'm sorry. That's why I haven't told anyone about her." Franics looked truly wretched.

"How long have you known her? Where did you meet her?" This news was dumbfounding to Julius. Francis had never even hinted that he was courting someone.

"Please, Jules. I…I cannot talk about it. Not now." His brother rose and refilled his glass, higher than before.

"As you wish. But you know I will do anything at all to help you with this or anything else, Francis." That the situation troubled his brother deeply made Julius vow to keep abreast of his brother's progress with his mysterious lady.

With a noncommittal shrug, Frances drank deeply, then quickly changed the subject. "Do you truly think Alex will be able to find and marry a woman in ten days?"

"Well, I'm certain he's undertaken forced marches before. I wouldn't put it past him." Julius chuckled "However, I may be able to give him a run for his money if my interview with Lord Tilney goes well." He grinned at the thought. "Perhaps I should write to him and give him fair warning that I intend to take a bride now as well."

August 29
Near Thetford
Norfolk, England

A WEEK LATER Julius stood before Lord Tilney's dark-mahogany desk, taking in the severe nature of the office with interest. The dark-oak-paneled walls, the sparce offerings of artwork, and the even darker drapery at the single window all impressed him that Lord Tilney wished to put forward the persona of a commanding gentleman who would brook no nonsense. Whether or not that façade depicted the true Lord Tilney, Julius would see. The gentleman had taught Lady Augusta the game of chess. These trappings might simply be his opening move with every business dealing—or suitor for his daughter's hand.

The earl's bushy eyebrows were puckered in a frown, making him look like an ogre from one of Andersen's fairy tales. Not an image one would wish to recall for his future father-in-law. Julius adjusted his perspective and smiled. "Good afternoon, my lord. Thank you for seeing me today."

"Lord Boxted, do have a seat." Lord Tilney motioned to one of the soft red-leather chairs that stood before the massive desk.

Julius lowered himself onto a wonderfully comfortable chair—the leather so soft he felt as though he was sitting on a cloud—and tried to relax. He had gone over the points he wished to make to persuade Lord Tilney to allow him to marry his daughter several times on the train this morning from London to Thetford until he had to stop the list from spilling out willy-nilly.

"Your letter said you had something to discuss with me regarding my daughter, Lady Augusta." The older gentleman peered at him from his higher perch on a chair that towered over the desk. "You were a guest at the house party this past April, were you not?"

"I was, my lord. That is when I first met Lady Augusta although we also met quite frequently during the Season as well." Julius tapped his finger against his leg until he realized he was showing his nervousness and stilled his hand. "During that time I became quite fond of the lady."

"If that is true, Boxted, why has it taken you this long to approach me?" The earl looked perturbed. "You are here to ask for her hand, are you not?"

"I am, Lord Tilney." Julius sat up straighter, his mouth in a grim line. "And I have not spoken to you before this because I was given to understand that the lady might have been previously affianced."

Lord Tilney reared back in his chair. "Did Lady Augusta tell you this?"

"I overheard her speaking of a possible betrothal to Miss Washer." With an effort, Julius refrained from making a fist. "I did not wish to overstep if the lady's affections lay with someone else."

"Bah." Lord Tilney rose suddenly, turning to a sideboard and poured out a splash of what looked to be brandy. "Had I known my daughter would become infatuated with Mr. Burton, I would not have invited him to dinner four years ago." He trained a keen eye on Julius. "Are you acquainted with Mr. Richard Burton, Boxted?"

"The explorer?" The name surprised Julius. "I am familiar with his exploits, although I have never been introduced to him. And you say this is the gentleman to whom Lady Augusta is betrothed?"

"Not betrothed, no." Tilney sipped his drink, musing. "They met here at dinner when she was just fifteen. He enthralled her with stories of Africa and that foolhardy trip to Mecca. My daughter has been sheltered all her life, and that circumstance has left her with a thirst for adventure, which Burton supplied with ease. After he left, she talked of nothing else and deviled me until

I'd bought his books for her to read."

"Did Mr. Burton declare for her?" Julius was on the edge of his seat.

Lord Tilney stared at him as though he was a lunatic. "Lady Augusta was fifteen years old at the time, Boxted. Burton looked on her as part of his adoring audience, nothing more."

"Then why does she believe he wishes to—"

"Because she wishes to believe it." He looked at the almost empty glass in his hand. "Would you like one?"

"Yes, please." Julius never wanted anything so much in his life.

"My daughter thinks she would like a life of adventure and sees Mr. Burton as her best hope of achieving it. I've tried to dissuade her, to explain she'd never enjoy such a life, but over the years she's convinced herself this is what she wants." Lord Tilney looked disgusted. "I've tried to make her see such a life for what it is, but she will not listen. And Burton doesn't help the matter by cutting such a dashing figure, with that scar on his cheek and that absurdly large mustache."

"He does present a romantic image, my lord." Much as Julius hated to admit it. "Has he given her any encouragement?"

"From time to time he writes to me, telling me about his most recent adventure and often he will either address a few lines to my daughter or he'll enclose a letter within mine to her. Nothing untoward." The earl hastened to make that point. "Still, it has given Lady Augusta false hope."

"You are certain it is false?" The lady had sounded very sure when speaking to her friend.

"Mr. Burton has been engaged to marry a Miss Arundell for several years now. Her family objects to the match—quite rightly I might add—but the betrothal has never been broken." Lord Tilney shook his head. "No, I cannot think he has any affection for my daughter past enjoying her adoration."

Julius rose, squeezing the glass with an iron fist. "Then will you give me your consent to court Lady Augusta, my lord? To marry her if she agrees?"

"Boxted, I am giving you my blessing in all your endeavors where my daughter is concerned. I will heartily approve if you can persuade her to forsake her ideas about Burton and marry you instead. I daresay you will not carry her off to the wilds of Borneo or some other God-forsaken place?"

"Borneo is unlikely, my lord." Julius knit his brows furiously. If the lady wished for tales of adventure, some of his escapades on his Grand Tour might interest her. He set his drink on the desk. "Perhaps I can make adventures closer to home seem as thrilling."

"You will have your work cut out for you, Boxted." He took a letter from the drawer of the desk and showed it to Julius. "I received this from Burton the day before yesterday. It includes a letter for Lady Augusta in which he talks of his return to England in the near future. I fear she will take that as a sign that he is coming to ask her to marry him."

"And you cannot conveniently lose that letter, can you, my lord?" Julius knew before he asked that the gentleman in Tilney would refuse to do something so dishonorable.

"Alas, I fear I cannot." The earl did look truly sorry about it. "Although I can hold this letter here until she comes home from Lord Caxton's house party this weekend. I don't expect her or my wife to arrive before Monday next. They are being detained in Hampshire due to the wedding on Friday."

"Whose wedding, my lord?" Julius's ears pricked up. His cousin Alex had gone to Lord Caxton's house party as well. And wagered he could marry by the end of the month.

"Miss Washer, who Lady Tilney sponsored this Season." The earl turned genial. "She's marrying Captain Bancroft, who is…" Lord Tilney ground to a halt.

"My cousin, yes, my lord." He might not have beaten Alex to wed first, but Alex quite likely had just helped him. "I hadn't been informed of the wedding."

"It came in today's post. You will likely have a letter waiting for you when you return to London." Tilney cocked his head. "Will you be attending?"

Nodding eagerly, Julius headed for the door. There wasn't a moment to lose. "Of course I will make every effort to attend, my lord." He bowed and pulled the door open. "Shall I give your regards to Lady Tilney and Lady Augusta for you?"

A smile spread over Lord Tilney's face. "I'd be much obliged if you would, Boxted." He nodded slightly. "Much obliged."

CHAPTER FIVE

August 31
Caxton Manor
Hampshire, England

STARING INTO THE mirror as Clarke put the finishing touches on her coiffure, Augusta sighed and tried not to feel bitter. She and her mother just watched her best friend marry a man she'd only just met when the house party had begun scarcely a week before. Not that she was jealous of her friend's choice of husband in Captain Alexander Bancroft. Augusta had had no designs of her own on the gentleman, to be sure. He was handsome enough and pleasant enough, and surely dashing enough for any young lady who delighted in a scarlet coat, but he hadn't interested Augusta in the least.

The problem was Augusta had known for years who she wanted to marry but was only slightly better off now than she had been when she'd first met Mr. Burton. At least now she was of an age to marry him. But she couldn't do anything about making that happen when he was off halfway around the world in the western part of America. So to watch Emma pluck a husband almost out of thin air was disconcerting in the extreme.

Of course, there were other options, if she would admit it. Several young gentlemen had stood out to her during the Season, the most likely of whom was Lord Boxted. They had met frequently at *ton* entertainments through May and June and he'd acquitted himself admirably on dance floors, in theater boxes, and on many stately garden walks. A pleasant and witty companion, he was head and shoulders above the rest of the gentlemen who'd shown an interest in her this year.

And still, she hadn't given him any true encouragement. Neither would she do so if she wished to avoid the dreary, predictable life her parents had led, that she'd led until now. Lord Boxted was heir to an earldom and with such a title came responsibilities and duties for him and his wife. Augusta would rather not have that burden fall upon her shoulders if she could marry someone like Mr. Burton instead. Life as the wife of an adventurer would have very different responsibilities, and much more freedom than she'd ever had before. If she had to bide her time and wait for Mr. Burton to return, then she would do so.

It didn't matter at all how attractive Lord Boxted had looked in the elegantly cut navy-blue suit he'd worn at his cousin's wedding today. Augusta's cheeks heated at the remembrance of seeing him in the congregation of the chapel once she'd walked down the aisle as Emma's maid of honor. She'd looked out at the sea of faces and immediately noted him in the third row. Her pulse had sped up and she'd become so hot, she'd thought she'd swoon. The reaction baffled her, although she supposed she could put it down to surprise. She'd not believed he'd be attending the wedding as he'd not been at the Caxton house party and the whole wedding had happened so quickly. But all of the Duke of Welwyn's grown grandsons had been present to congratulate Captain Alexander Bancroft on his marriage to Emma.

She'd not spoken to Lord Boxted at the wedding breakfast. After her strange reaction at the wedding, she'd thought it best that she not meet him. Instead she'd spent most of the time with Emma, trying to pry the mystery of how she and Captain Bancroft had broken the garden swing out of her.

How she'd manage to avoid Lord Boxted at dinner tonight

and afterward, she hadn't a clue. Perhaps he wouldn't wish to speak to her, or if he did, she might feel nothing untoward. Her giddiness this morning could have been brought on by being anxious about her role in the wedding.

"Is that to your liking, my lady?" Clarke stood back and Augusta glanced at her hair, swept up into a mass of ringlet curls atop her head with small pink and green artificial flowers fixed here and there with a charming randomness.

"Excellent as always, Clarke. Thank you." Augusta rose and the maid draped an ivory, red, and green paisley shawl around her shoulders. Her pale green silk gown with pink rosettes scattered over it wasn't one of her favorites, but it did become her very well, making her skin a perfect ivory and bringing out the blue of her eyes. She actually preferred bolder colors, although her mother kept admonishing her that such hues were for married ladies only. The result was a struggle anytime they visited the modiste. Augusta had agreed to the ordering of the pastel-colored gowns only because, in exchange, her mother had promised she could have several made in deeper colors, even one in the deep-gold color she adored.

Heading down to the drawing room where the guests had been gathering before dinner, Augusta raised her chin, resolving to spend the meal talking to her mother about their plans for the autumn. The Little Season was upon them, and although she believed her mother wished her to attend it, Augusta now wished to persuade her to wait until they knew when Mr. Burton would return to England.

She entered the drawing room and immediately headed toward her mother, meaning to ask if there had been a letter from her father. He might even now know something about Mr. Burton's plans.

"Lady Augusta."

She stopped dead still, the voice of Lord Boxted sending a thrill down her spine. Turning toward him, she couldn't stop herself from smiling at the sight of the handsome gentleman, flawlessly attired in his evening dress and looking even more dashing than she remembered him from their last encounter at Lady Tupperfield's soiree.

"Lord Boxted, how do you do?" She curtsied, her heart giving a strange little skip.

"I am very well, my lady." His eyes snapped with merriment. "I hope you are, as well? Have you enjoyed your time at Lord and Lady Caxton's house party?"

"I have, my lord." She shifted from foot to foot, making her belled skirts sway. "It has been quite thrilling to see my friend Miss Washer married so quickly. She only just met Captain Bancroft a week ago."

"Alex is a fortunate man. Miss Washer is a charming young lady, although I suppose I should now say Mrs. Bancroft is a charming woman." He grinned. "I hope they will be truly happy."

"I am surprised to see you here, my lord." That hadn't been the topic she'd intended to broach, but it had come out, nevertheless.

"Really?" His brows rose alarmingly. "You know me better than that, Lady Augusta. You know family is most important to the Quartermains—almost as important as wagering."

She laughed at that and relaxed a bit. Why he was making her nervous tonight she had no idea. "Yes, I do know that, my lord. But the wedding came about so quickly, I scarcely thought anyone would be in attendance."

"A train journey of a few hours from London is nothing an enterprising gentleman couldn't arrange." He motioned toward his cousins, clustered around their grandfather. "You see we have all managed to turn out." His gaze slid back to her, his eyes intent on her face. "Are you happy to see me here, my lady?"

Augusta's heart gave a great thump, so loud she feared he could hear it. She threw a panic-stricken glance around the room and was relieved that the butler had just opened the door to the dining room. "I think we are about to go in, my lord."

Without taking his gaze off her, he offered his arm. "I was

told I was to escort you in, my lady."

Nodding, she took his arm. The matter of precedence would of course dictate their seating. And as their ranks were of a similar standing, it was understandable he would be her dinner partner. As they filed in, finding their correct place in the throng of guests, Augusta couldn't help wondering if the Fates were trying to take a hand in deciding her future.

As Julius led Lady Augusta to their seats midway down the table, he tried to keep a firm grip on his plan for this evening's dinner. Based on her father's information about Mr. Burton's influence on Lady Augusta, Julius had used his time on the trains the past few days to devise a plan to demonstrate to the lady that even though he wasn't an adventurer per se, he'd traveled a good bit of the world and had had his share of exploits. He only hoped Burton's explorations were what had fascinated Lady Augusta and not some other quality or characteristic about the man.

Once they were seated, he dropped his napkin in his lap and turned to Lady Augusta, a smile on his lips. "Do you know where the bride and groom are off to for their wedding trip?"

Lady Augusta shook her head and took up her water glass. "Captain Bancroft is stationed in London at present, awaiting his next posting. So they are traveling there until he's given his orders."

"The military life certainly gives one the opportunity to travel the world." His cousin had said that many times, and it was true enough. If you didn't mind going somewhere you didn't wish to go.

"Mrs. Bancroft shouldn't mind following the drum. She's used to traveling long distances. She was in India with her aunt and uncle for some time." Lady Augusta got a distant look in her eyes.

"Would you like to see India, my lady?"

She turned to him, a pucker to her lips. "I would like to see any place outside of England or Scotland, my lord. I've not had the opportunity to do so, so far. Although I have hopes that that may change soon."

"Indeed, are you planning a trip?" Julius kept the question light, despite his knowledge to the contrary.

"Not planning one, so much as I hope to be invited to travel soon." She turned back to her place as the soup was served.

"Well, if you have any say in the matter, I will suggest you visit Italy, and Naples in particular, although you might prefer Venice. The shopping is quite wonderful there." He tasted the soup, which was delicious, and waited to see if she would rise to the bait.

"Why did you prefer Naples?" Her delicate brows rose slightly. "If the shopping was better elsewhere."

"Because Naples is only a short carriage ride from the excavation at Pompeii."

"Pompeii?" She turned to him, her eyes wide. "You were allowed to visit the excavation?"

"As my grandfather is a duke, his letter of introduction to Signor Spinelli, the current director of the museum and excavation, worked wonders." It had been a very fortunate introduction, as few people other than archeologists were usually allowed at the dig.

"What was is like?" He'd never seen such a rapt look on Lady Augusta's face outside of the times they'd met over a chessboard. "Were you actually able to walk the streets of the city?"

"Yes, I was." He sipped his wine, remembering the awe he'd felt when standing on the newly uncovered stone walkways. "I walked over the area called the Forum, saw all the ancient Roman columns standing guard around it, with Mount Vesuvius sitting there, ever present in the distance. It was a chilling sight."

"How fortunate you were, my lord." Lady Augusta sounded humbled. "I have read several works that talk about the excavation as well as Mr. Bulwer-Lytton's *The Last Days of Pompeii*, but to actually have been there and walked the streets would be a dream come true."

"You are a student of history, my lady?"

She shook her head. "No, but I am an aficionado of adventure. To go where others have not been before, or to see those places and things that most people can only dream of or read about..." A wistful look came over her face. "I will admit this moment I am extremely jealous of you, Lord Boxted. You have done so much more already than I can scarcely ever aspire to doing."

"I would think, Lady Augusta, that you will find a way to make your dreams come true." Julius watched her, suddenly overcome with the need to comfort her. "If any lady can mold her destiny, I would wager it is you."

Her smile lit up her face. "If you would wager on me, my lord, I think I must take heart." Then the light went out of her eyes. "But for a woman, it all depends on who she marries as to what her life will be like. My parents, for example, had an arranged marriage and it has suited my mother well from what I can tell. Being the Countess of Tilney is all she ever wished to be." Her face shifted, defiance in every line. "However, that is not all I wish for myself, my lord."

"I would never think that, my lady." And yet if he managed to get Lady Augusta to agree to marry him, wouldn't that be her lot in life? Would he be caging a bird that would only ever want its freedom? "I hope you are able to find a way to realize every dream you wish for yourself."

"You are very kind, my lord." She drank some wine, then turned to him again. "Where else did you travel to? You were on your Grand Tour when you visited Pompeii?"

"Yes, I was. I began in France, in Paris, then went through Switzerland down into Italy." From the hunger in her eyes, Julius almost didn't want to tell her the ultimate stop on his journey. "And then, on a whim, I took a ship from Naples to Egypt."

"You have been to Egypt?" The disbelief in her voice was almost more than Julius could bear. "You have seen the pyramids? The Sphynx?"

He nodded, again watching her intently.

"Oh, Lord Boxted. You have been holding out on me all this time." The delight on her face enabled Julius to breathe again. "You simply must tell me—"

"My dear Lady Augusta." Lord Sherborne, her dinner partner on her right, had turned to her, his face eager. "You must tell me about your father's estate in Scotland. He's invited me to come up next month for the shooting and I thought I would find out the lay of the land, so to speak, from you, dear lady."

They had come to the end of the first course, at which point etiquette demanded that those of polite society must turn and make conversation with the dinner partner on their other side. Lady Augusta gave him one stricken look, then obediently turned toward Lord Sherborne and began to relate a description of her father's hunting estate in the Highlands.

Just as disappointed, Julius dutifully turned to the elderly lady on his left. "Lady Corby, how did you enjoy the wedding?"

At least now, having gotten his partner started on a topic he was certain she could speak about for the entire main course, Julius allowed part of his mind to mull over everything he'd just discovered about Lady Augusta. Paramount, it seemed, was her desire for travel and adventure. At least those were desires he could easily satisfy if they were married. They could take an extended wedding trip to rival his Grand Tour. He could show her Paris and Pompeii, Venice and Napoli, and Egypt in all its magnificent splendor. Nothing could be easier.

What he couldn't do was promise her she would never have to become the Countess of Winwick, with all the duties and responsibilities that station entailed. When she married him, that too would become her destiny. Could she come to love him enough that their early life of excitement and adventure could compensate her for her eventual role as countess?

Julius had no idea if Lady Augusta had any sort of affection or feeling for him past their current friendship, although he did believe they had forged that much. As there was so much to admire about the lady, for his part he could easily see himself falling in love. They had the Little Season before them, providing plenty of opportunities for them to deepen their acquaintance. And if Mr. Burton would kindly keep himself out of the country this autumn, then perhaps Julius could bring the lady around. Unfortunately, on this particular wager, even he didn't like his odds for success.

CHAPTER SIX

December 7
Ashford, Kent, England

K ICKING HIMSELF FOR being a fool once again, Julius stood at the edge of the Kastner's ballroom floor gazing across it at Lady Augusta endeavoring once more to avoid making eye contact with him. In truth, he couldn't blame her. Who would wish to gaze at the gentleman who had deviled you the entire Little Season with proposals you did not wish to hear? He'd badly miscalculated Lady Augusta's depth of affection for Mr. Burton— or her decision not to become a countess—so much so he wouldn't take no for an answer to his proposal—all five times.

It was as though he'd lost at chess using the King's Gambit with Lady Augusta, then instead of trying other strategies, he'd decided that if he kept making the same mistake over and over, eventually she'd grow tired and simply give up and concede the game. Needless to say that had not happened. And yet, he'd not been able to stop himself from proposing.

If only Francis had shown sense and locked him up in his room at home. Or dragged him off to America until he came to his senses. Things might have been salvageable between him and Lady Augusta then.

"You have met my older daughter, Miss St. Claire, have you

not, Lord Boxted?" Smiling cheerfully, Mrs. St. Claire broke in on Julius's thoughts, having just joined him as he stood alone before the orchestra began to tune up.

"We have not been formally introduced, no, ma'am." Julius forced himself to refocus his attention or try to, at least, for the sake of Miss St. Claire. No need to appear rude even if he were the stupidest man in all of England.

"Dear Charlotte has been so looking forward to her come out in the Spring." Mrs. St. Claire looked up at him eagerly.

With an internal sigh, he smiled pleasantly. He must get used to the matchmaking mamas he'd encounter in the spring. Not only would the *ton* be twittering about his eligible status, but news of the family's marriage wager would bring them out in droves. Another thing he could have avoided if he'd been able to get Lady Augusta to agree to marry him. "I am certain she will be a diamond of the first water, Mrs. St. Claire."

The lady in question was indeed quite as pretty as the proverbial English rose. Her cheeks were a soft-pink color, one associated with delicate flowers, her skin then blending into a creamy ivory. Her eyes were the color of the blue willow china pattern his mother used for tea sometimes. The lady's blond hair was dressed simply in a braid coiled around her head and enclosed with a circlet of gold filigree and pearls. The classic bow of her pink lips was utterly perfect.

However, other than an admiration for the ideal of English womanhood, Miss St. Claire moved Julius not at all. When one had been thinking of nothing save the raven-haired ringlets of a statuesque lady who had the mien and manner of a goddess, one did not instantaneously change his tune and seek a less robust one. At least Julius didn't. Still, that did not mean he could not be polite and ask the young lady to dance.

Affecting a warm smile, Julius turned to his companion and asked, "Would you please introduce me to your eldest daughter, Mrs. St. Claire?"

The woman's eyebrows shot straight up. "Of course, my

lord." She hastily motioned to the young lady who hurried over to them. "Charlotte, may I present Lord Boxted, who has especially asked for an introduction to you." Her smile widened to rival a crocodile's. "This is my daughter, my lord, Miss St. Claire."

"How do you do, Miss St. Claire." Julius bowed to the young lady, who smiled shyly back at him.

"I am very well, my lord. I am delighted to make your acquaintance." The lady *did* look delighted. "My mother told me your family and mine were friends when we were last in England."

"Yes, my grandmother reminded me of the connection last evening." His grandmother had summoned him to her chamber at home as soon as the invitation to the house party arrived and informed him of the long friendship between their families and charged him specifically to be cordial to the St. Claires—to *all* the St. Claires. Yet another matchmaking mamma, or grandmother in this case, he suspected.

"I remember playing with your cousins when I was young. Iphigenia was my bosom friend." Miss St. Claire grinned at the memory.

"My sisters are a bit younger than Iphigenia, Cassandra, and Phaedra, but I am certain you would enjoy their company as well."

Miss St. Claire's eyes glowed with a soft light, giving Julius the impression she was a very agreeable young lady. Rather a pity he preferred more spirited ones. "I'm certain I will enjoy making their acquaintance now that we are back in England."

"If you are not engaged for the next dance, Miss St. Claire, I would be delighted to claim it."

"Thank you, my lord." The lady's smile widened. "It is not taken—except now it is, by you." She giggled, a charming sound, to be sure, but a little of it would be sufficient.

"I wonder if it will be a waltz? I love a waltz." Julius glanced over at the orchestra, hoping they would strike up the music soon. He couldn't help but remember the waltzes he and Lady Augusta had danced at all the entertainments during the Season. He sighed. One must move on.

Almost reflectively he glanced over the dance floor to the spot where Lady Augusta stood—and met with that lady's indignant glare.

Julius's first reaction was to glance around to make sure he was the correct recipient of the lady's anger. But he was the only person in the vicinity, save Mrs. St. Claire and her daughter. And with that realization, Julius's spirits rose for the first time in weeks. Perhaps, just perhaps, there was a chance she hadn't quite decided against him after all.

A triumphant smile touched his lips, and he offered his arm to his partner. "I believe the orchestra is about to begin. Shall we take the floor, Miss St. Claire?"

"With pleasure, my lord."

"I fear we are not going to get our waltz, Miss St. Claire, but I daresay a reel will give us as much pleasure."

"I suspect it will, my lord." She squeezed his hand and leaned against his arm.

Julius couldn't resist shooting a glance toward Lady Augusta and was rewarded with a return gaze through narrowed eyes that was likely meant to singe his eyebrows off. Chuckling to himself, Julius patted his partner's hand.

The chessboard had just been reset. Time to implement a new strategy.

THE SCOTTISH REEL had scarcely finished before Julius whisked Miss St. Clair back to her mother and scanned the dance floor to locate Lady Augusta. She'd not been in the group of eight with Julius and his partner, which was a good thing. They both might have been too self-conscious dancing together but with different partners.

He spied her standing with Fritz Kastner and a young lady he'd seen earlier out in the woods gathering greenery. With studied nonchalance, he strolled over to them, taking care that Lady Augusta didn't see him approaching. The plan was to surprise her with his presence, then assure her he was not about to propose again.

"What are you doing?" His cousin Tom Weston grabbed his arm and towed him over to a corner of the room.

"Let me go." He shrugged his arm out of Tom's grasp. "I was about to ask Lady Augusta to dance."

"Are you sure that's *all* you were about to ask her?" His cousin gave him a sour look.

"It was. I have no intention of asking her to marry me to-night." What he might do later on was none of Tom's business.

"I had strict instructions from Francis not to let you within ten feet of Lady Augusta." Tom crossed his arms over his chest, looking like Julius would have to tunnel through him.

"For God's sake, I am not going to ask her for anything save a dance." Julius had had enough. "Let me by, cousin, or I swear I will chuck you out on the verandah."

"No, thank you. I just came in from an altercation with Yule out there. It's damned cold outside." Tom shook his head. "All right, but I'm following you over to Lady Augusta and if you so much as look like you're about to go down on one knee, I'm hauling you outside."

"Done." Julius side-stepped around Tom and continued to-ward Lady Augusta, his cousin at his heels. They reached the lady, who had been talking to Fritz and his companion, and so fortunately had not noted their approach.

"Good evening, Lady Augusta, Fritz." Julius looked enquir-ingly at Fritz. "Who is this lovely lady?"

"Agatha," he said, addressing the short, dark-haired lady in the deep lavender gown, "this is my friend Lord Boxted. He's Yule's cousin. This is my sister, Miss Kastner. She's the youngest, and the last of my sisters to become engaged. This house party is in honor of her betrothal to Baron von Lippe."

"Felicitations to you, Miss Kastner." Julius bowed, careful to keep his attention on the lady. A look at either Lady Augusta or his cousin would be disastrous. "My very best wishes for your happiness."

"Thank you, Lord Boxted." Miss Kastner dipped a curtsey but gave her brother a speaking look.

"Mine as well, Miss Kastner." Tom mumbled absently, looking at Julius like a cat sitting in front of a mouse hole about to pounce.

"If you will excuse me, Lady Augusta and gentlemen, I must take Agatha to her next partner. The dancing is about to begin again." With a hasty bow, Fritz shepherded his sister to the far side of the ballroom.

Julius turned immediately to Lady Augusta, who looked as though she wished to flee with her host. "Lady Augusta, as the orchestra is about to strike up, I wondered if you would do me the honor of dancing the next with me?"

Both Lady Augusta and his cousin turned to him, their mouths slightly open.

Biting back a laugh, Julius waited, gazing at the lady evenly. He'd wager he had a fifty-fifty chance of her agreeing.

"You wish only for a dance, my lord?" She stared directly into his face, that familiar puckered look on her lips.

"That is all, my lady." Julius looked at her evenly and held his breath.

"If you are certain that is all, then yes, I would be happy to dance the next with you." The smile she gave him then was genuine and lit up her face as nothing else had for a long time.

"I believe my work is done here." Tom grinned at Julius and slapped him on the back. "Don't go getting into trouble, cousin. My lady." He bowed, then made a beeline for the doorway, likely gone in search of a libation.

If the orchestra hadn't been tuning up, Julius would have

gone with him. A drink to steady his nerves would be appreciated right now. He offered his arm. "Shall we take the dance floor, Lady Augusta. I do believe we may be in for a treat."

"What do you mean?"

"I believe they are going to play a waltz." Julius led her onto the floor, then assumed the position, with one of his hands grasping hers, the other one firmly resting on her back and waist. It was the sole reason he loved dancing this with Lady Augusta, being able to touch her so intimately, almost holding her in his arms.

The music began—a popular waltz by Strauss—and Julius swept her away, twirling them effortlessly around the dance floor. Dancing had always come effortlessly to him, the rhythm of the music with its mathematical precision creating an instantaneous connection between his mind and the rest of his body. He scarcely had to think of anything at all, except in this instance, his partner's beautiful face.

Lady Augusta wore an expression of calm reserve to begin with, likely because she still expected him to attempt another proposal. Nothing could have been further from his mind, and about halfway through the dance, her face and body relaxed and she began to enjoy the dance as she had the many times they'd partnered at balls during the Season. So now it was time for him to speak. "Thank you for forgiving me, my lady."

"Forgiving you for what, Lord Boxted?" A wary look crept into her face.

"For annoying you so dreadfully this past autumn with my unwarranted and unwelcome spate of proposals." He dipped and whirled them around, positioning them farther from the orchestra so it would be easier to talk.

"How do you know I've forgiven you?" A look of pique flared in her eyes.

"You are dancing with me, my lady. And now speaking to me, which you have not done for some time." He grinned down at her. "I take that as forgiveness, whether it was meant as such or not."

Her lips puckered, and she glanced away. "You vexed me almost beyond patience, Lord Boxted. A sensible gentleman would have taken my reply of 'No, thank you,' as a definitive answer after the third time it had been rendered."

"I suppose I am not to be considered sensible then, Lady Augusta. At least not where you are concerned."

She shot him a wary look and her body tensed in his arms.

"I have, however, seen the error of my ways and promise to importune you no further with my unwelcome declarations." He gazed into the deep blue eyes, hopelessly ensnared by them. "I would instead beg that you allow us to remain friends."

"Friends?" Her brows furrowed in that delightfully charming way of hers. "How do you mean?"

"The way we were this past summer. I quite enjoyed the entertainments we attended and always looked forward to meeting you at them. I thought you did so as well." He chuckled. "Do you recall Lady Lavendon's theatre party at the Lyceum?"

Lady Augusta nodded, laughing. "The poor lady thought we were going to see a comedy."

"Apparently, she was not a fan of Mr. Dickens's works or she would have known *A Tale of Two Cities* was anything but comedic." They had actually laughed through parts of the tragic work because the lady kept loudly bemoaning the fact that she'd been misinformed about the subject of the play each time the plot took a tragic turn. "Will you be in Town for the Christmas pantomimes? If so, perhaps over the holidays I can persuade my mother to get up a party. There will certainly be no tragedy in *The Adventures of Mother Goose* or *Robinson Crusoe* or *The Harlequin Friday*."

Biting her lip, Lady Augusta shook her head. "I am not certain what plans my family has for the holidays. Nothing has been fixed as we are waiting for…" She paused, as if wanting to choose her words carefully. "We are unsure if we will have a guest this year. Once that is settled, I will know more." She peered into his face, a softness in her eyes. "But thank you for thinking of such a pleasant excursion. That is kind of you, my lord."

The prospective guest must be Burton, curse him, apparently not yet returned from America. Well, Julius wasn't about to let the absent suitor have it all his way. "Then allow me to beg you to come sleighing with me tomorrow morning. I do not believe there is any fixed activity for the guests, so I am certain Fritz can arrange it for us."

"That does sound lovely, my lord." Lady Augusta sounded excited by the prospect. "I do love the cold, crisp air. And the snow always makes the landscape look like a fairyland."

The last strains of the waltz faded and reluctantly Julius released his partner and bowed. "Splendid. May I escort you to your mother? Then I will search out Fritz and make all the arrangements."

"Very well, Lord Boxted." She took his arm before he could offer it, an action that sent a thrill through him. "Thank you so much for the lovely waltz." She smiled up at him. "I must admit, you have always been my favorite partner for a dance. I am never afraid you will put a foot wrong on the dance floor."

"Just on every other floor." Julius gave the words a rueful tone.

She laughed and tossed her head. "Hopefully, that is no longer true."

They arrived at Lady Tilney, who looked shocked to see her daughter on Julius's arm.

"Good evening, my lord. I did not know Lady Augusta was…dancing with you." She smiled warmly at him. "I would not have worried had I known."

Another ally perhaps. God knew he needed every one. "Good evening, my lady. So good to see you again. Lady Augusta has agreed to go sleighing with me tomorrow, so I must go arrange it with our host, if you will excuse me." He relinquished Lady Augusta's arm, reluctantly but with the hope of more to come on the morrow. "I will meet you in the foyer after breakfast then, my lady."

"I will be there, my lord." She sounded happy, which filled his heart with joy for the first time in weeks. He would get little sleep tonight anticipating tomorrow's outing with her.

"Good evening, ladies." Julius bowed and hurried away before he said something that would destroy the fragile truce he'd managed to create. So he could live to fight another day.

CHAPTER SEVEN

T HE NEXT MORNING, Augusta stood in the foyer surprisingly early, ready to meet Lord Boxted. She'd breakfasted first thing, then gone back upstairs to change her gown once more. Last evening, she'd originally planned to wear a heavy silk of deep blue with lighter-blue piping, but upon reflection, feared it might not be warm enough. So this morning, in consultation with her maid, she'd dressed in a buff-colored gown of merino wool. After breakfast, however she'd come to the conclusion the color did not suit her at all, and hurried back upstairs, calling for Turner as she rushed toward her chamber. The deep mauve gown of terry velvet, covered with her sable-trimmed carriage jacket and matching fur muff, would have to do as there was no time to change yet again. But Augusta was happy with this choice. The colors harmonized and the additional exercise had brought bright spots of color to her cheeks. She was quite ready to meet Lord Boxted.

"Good morning, my lady." His voice behind her sent a pleasant thrill of anticipation down her back.

She turned and smiled at him. "Good morning, my lord." Dressed for the cold as well, in a gray overcoat and tall beaver hat, Lord Boxted looked incredibly handsome. "It looks to be an excellent morning for a sleigh ride. Tate here," he nodded toward the Kastners' butler standing beside the door, "says the weather is crisp and cold, but no sign of another snow."

"Then we are most fortunate." Lord Boxted hurried down the steps and offered her his arm. "Do you know the neighborhood at all?"

"No. My parents are friends of the Kastners, but this is the first time I've been here in Kent." She'd been happy to add another county to her meager list of travels.

"Then I think you will be in for a treat." He handed her into the two-person sleigh, black with gold trim and red upholstery, as the groom held the horse's head. "I'll take you around part of the estate, then head toward Ashford, and come back around by the river."

"It sounds lovely." She tucked her gown in snugly as he walked around and climbed in the other side. Once he took his seat, Augusta realized just how tiny this sleigh was. Lord Boxted was pressed right up against her side. A quickened pulse began to beat in her veins.

Lord Boxted gathered the reins, nodded to the groom who released the tall bay gelding, then clicked to the horse who started forward at a walk. Another click and the animal moved into a fast-paced trot, taking them down the driveway handily. The stark trees and snowy landscape sped by, silently save for the merry jingling of the horse's bells. Although Augusta had been on sleigh rides before, this one had the added air of adventure to it. Possibly because of the gentleman driving the sleigh.

"Do you drive, my lady?" he asked when they turned onto the smooth as glass road.

"No, I never learned. I do ride, of course, but for some reason I never drove even a pony cart." Odd that she hadn't ever thought of doing such a thing. She believed ladies often did drive themselves.

"I would be happy to teach you." He glanced over at her. "Not today, of course. You should learn in a cart or carriage on dry land. But perhaps this summer," he stared hard at her, "if you are in London again."

He meant if she wasn't married by then.

"Thank you, my lord." Augusta nodded, suddenly wishing Mr. Burton had already arrived and her wait was over. If he didn't propose… She'd never allowed herself to believe he wouldn't, or that she wouldn't find a way to make him propose to her. A surreptitious glance at Lord Boxted showed his face in magnificent profile in the morning sun. The smooth brow, straight nose, and strong jaw proclaimed him every bit as dashing as Mr. Burton. Even without a mustache.

She'd admit she'd missed the companionship they'd had during the Season more than a little. Even though he'd been beyond annoying with his incessant proposals during the fall. Still, she enjoyed his company immensely—as long as he wasn't asking to marry her. No matter how much she admired him, she couldn't allow herself to marry a gentleman who would expect her to lead the unexceptional life her mother had. Augusta wanted more than that and not even the fast beating of her heart when she carried out a spirited banter with Lord Boxted was going to change that.

"We are rounding the edge of the Kastners' estate here. That stone wall demarks his property." Lord Boxted nodded to an ancient, crumbling wall half buried in the snow.

"You know the area quite well, my lord."

"I spent some holidays here with Fritz when we were in university together." He laughed. "He liked showing off his property and the surroundings and I paid attention."

"Then whose estate borders his?" She sat up, eager to challenge him.

"Do you mean to test my faculties, my lady?" He shook his head then turned to stare at her. "A bold move when I could simply invent an answer and you would not know if I am correct or not."

"But I can ask Mr. Kastner when we return, my lord." She raised her chin. "And then I would know if you were false or not."

"Once again, you are too clever for me, Lady Augusta." He chuckled and returned his gaze to the road. "And the answer to your question is the MacGregor family. They have the property next to Fritz. If you look through that cluster of trees," he pointed to the right, "you should be able to see the manor house."

Augusta peered through the stand of black trees and caught a glimpse of a substantial residence. "I can see it. It's quite impressive."

They rounded a curve in the road and were suddenly flanked on both sides by massive forests, spindly trees standing like tall, dark soldiers. In the distance, a dog began to bark.

"This road will take us into the market town of Ashford. If the shops are open, we could stop if you are in need of anything." He looked over inquiringly.

"A lady is forever in need of ribbons or gloves, my lord. You should know that." Augusta's ears perked up. "Do you hear something?"

"Just the dog barking. Why?" He cocked his head. "What do you hear?"

"Thunder." Even as she said it Augusta thought herself a fool. She looked up into a clear blue cloudless sky. Still, there was a rumbling noise coming from somewhere. "You don't hear that?"

He paused, listening, and frowned. "There is something. If that infernal hound would stop baying—"

With a shocking suddenness, the thunderous pounding became deafening as a huge stag burst out of the woods to their right, not ten feet in front of them, hotly pursued by the baying dog.

The startled horse jibbed and reared, neighing as his hooves pawed at the air.

Augusta couldn't repress a scream as the sleigh slid sideways, almost landing them in a ditch.

The stag continued into the forest on the opposite side of the road, the dog hotly on its heels as the horse's hooves came down on the icy road with a huge thump. It took off at a gallop, the sleigh skidding wildly across the road.

Heart in her throat, Augusta pushed her muff up her arm and gripped the side of the sleigh for dear life as they raced down the frozen road. Lord Boxted's arms were taut, his fingers tugging on the reins steadily in an effort to pull the horse back down, but the animal was too spooked to obey any command. They dashed down the country road, the landscape rushing by in a dizzying blur. Augusta kept her gaze trained on Lord Boxted, praying he could bring them to a safe stop.

With a calmness Augusta would never have believed, he braced his feet against the footboard of the sleigh and stood up. His tall black hat flew off his head, but he didn't seem to notice as he concentrated on bringing all his weight and strength to bear on the reins. His death-grip on the leather ribbons never slackened, giving Augusta hope that he could gain control of the animal.

The road, however, curved suddenly as the terrain rose into steep banks. The crazed horse still refused to slow and Augusta braced herself for disaster. They took the turn at an incredible speed, the runners of the sleigh veering uncontrollably as they slammed into the left-hand bank and bounced back onto the road. The jolt threw Lord Boxted into her, but he righted himself immediately, pulling violently on the reins and shouting, "Whoa!"

Miraculously, either his shout or the fearsome tug seemed to affect the horse. Bit by bit the animal slowed until at last they came to a complete stop in the middle of the snowy road.

Lord Boxted plopped back down into the seat beside her, staring straight ahead and puffing as though he'd run every step alongside the horse.

Heart hammering in her chest, Augusta sat panting also, looking around as though she'd never seen the world before. Gulping in deep breaths of the cold air, she slowly pried her hands from the side of the sleigh. Even then they shook uncontrollably, and she pulled her muff down over them so Lord Boxted couldn't see. Dazed, she turned toward him and in a shaky voice said,

"Thank you, my lord."

Slowly, he turned toward her, his face pale, his eyes almost black. He stared at her for half a moment, then leaned forward, grasped her face, and kissed her.

Already stunned, Augusta could scarcely register the shock. Lord Boxted was actually kissing her! What on earth did he think he was doing?

Whatever it was, he was doing it very, very well. His lips on hers were firm, commanding, absolutely giving no quarter. To her astonishment, she reveled in his complete mastery over her. He pressed harder against her lips, his tongue emerging to seek entry. Augusta didn't exactly understand that request, but she knew the answer he sought. Unable to resist, she opened her mouth and he slid his tongue inside.

Compared to the shocks of the past quarter hour, his move scarcely raised an eyebrow. Instead, she slid her arms around his shoulders, pulling him closer to her. Then she gave herself over to him fully, delighting as he plundered here and there, drinking deeply of these new sensations, of sharing this very intimate moment with the gentleman she realized she no longer wished to refuse.

That thought acted like a snowball splattering in her face. She gasped and pulled back, staring at Lord Boxted as though she'd never seen him before. Had he changed or had she? In an effort to regain control of herself and keep him at arm's length until she could sort out this plethora of new feelings, she said the first thing that came into her head. "Are you trying to compromise me, my lord?"

Lord Boxted blew out a breath, ran his hand through his windblown hair, and pursed his lips. "If I'd wanted to do that, Lady Augusta, I'd have kissed you somewhere where there were witnesses." He looked pointedly around the silent road. "I do not think the horse is going to talk."

Augusta fought to keep from laughing and settled for a choked "Humm."

"Do not fear. Our secret is safe with me." Once more he ran his hand through his hair. "I seem to have lost my hat."

"It blew off when you stood up to try to control the horse." She looked at the road behind them, but there was nothing but snow. "Should we go back and find it?"

Shaking his head, he gathered the reins. "Not this minute. It will be impossible to turn the sleigh around on this narrow track. Best to stick to the plan and continue into Ashford. We can turn around there easily, and then head back to the Kastners'. If we are lucky, we may retrieve my hat on the way back." He clicked to the horse who immediately began a sedate trot. "I think that will be enough excitement for one day, don't you?"

"For the rest of the month, my lord. Or the rest of the year." Augusta wanted to return to the house so she could sit before the fire in her chamber with a hot cup of tea and think about everything that had transpired today. "Where did you learn to handle horses like that? Your driving skills are certainly impressive."

"I've been riding since the age of three when I demanded to be put on a pony." Lord Boxted chuckled. "When I was eight, I graduated to a pony cart and I've been driving ever since."

"Have you ever had a horse bolt like that before?" If he hadn't had any experience, then he'd done an extraordinary job just now.

"I've had a saddle horse bolt and brought him under control, but never in a sleigh or even a carriage." Lord Boxted slowed the horse down to a walk as they came to the main thoroughfare of the town. "I'd say it's easier to control your horse from his back, because you are closer to the animal and have more direct contact. But that may be the wisdom of the years since that incident occurred speaking."

"Whatever it is, I must say thank you again for saving me. Us." She stared straight ahead as they made a circle around the town fountain and headed back out the road they had come in on. After today's demonstration of his masculine prowess, she had to admit she might have been mistaken about Lord Boxted. Perhaps he did measure up to Mr. Burton's mark.

"I am happy to have been of service, my lady." He said nothing else until they had left Ashford and were headed back toward the Kastners' estate. Once they were flying down the snowy road again, Lord Boxted glanced at her. "I wanted to say that I'm sorry about…the other thing as well, my lady."

"The other thing?" She knew full well what he was referring to, but she had to pretend ignorance for decency's sake.

"The kiss, my lady. I beg your pardon for taking advantage of the moment."

"The moment after you saved my life?" Was he sorry that he'd done it, or was he merely being polite? Because to judge by that kiss—and admittedly she had nothing else to compare it to—she had to think he was now being polite when in actuality he hadn't been sorry at all. She hoped he hadn't been sorry. She certainly wasn't.

"Yes, well, gentlemen can become…worked up after a fight or after a sporting contest or after saving a fair heroine from certain death." He grinned when he said it, but his eyes were serious. "I didn't want you to take it as a mark of disrespect. I have the utmost respect for you, Lady Augusta."

Respect was all well and good, however that kiss had left her wanting more from Lord Boxted. Perhaps ladies got worked up as well after nearly being killed. Her pulse had yet to return to a normal beat and if Lord Boxted kissed her like that again, well…she might very well kiss him back. "I didn't take it as disrespect, my lord." Far from it. "I suppose I thought of it as a celebration of…" She slid her gaze away from him, suddenly shy.

"Of what?"

She wrung her hands within her muff, not knowing what to say. "Of triumph."

"I suppose that is true."

She jerked her head toward him to find him grinning.

"Considering last evening I wasn't certain you'd ever speak to me again, I'd say today has been quite the triumph." He continued to grin, though he kept his eyes on the road. "And that triumph has made me bold once more."

Augusta's heart, which had almost quieted, took off racing like the startled horse. Dear lord, he was going to do it again. He was going to propose to her even though he'd expressly promised he would not. She drew herself up, summoning her indignation in order to upbraid him for breaking his promise, when the realization struck her as though she'd run full tilt into a stone wall. She *wanted* him to propose to her again. Because she wished to accept him.

Even though she'd not heard from Mr. Burton, the man had had plenty of chances, in the various letters he'd written to her, to make an offer and never had. And while she would give anything to live the life of an explorer's wife, other gentlemen possessed those same adventurous qualities. Lord Boxted possessed them, she'd wager her fortune on it. And although the rest of her life might not consist of jungle treks or journeys to India, she could believe that life with Lord Boxted would not be dull.

Summoning every shred of poise she still possessed, she looked at Lord Boxted and smiled innocently. "How so, my lord?"

"Well, I hope you will consider the question I wish to ask you in the spirit of close friendship that I believe we now possess."

"Yes?" Augusta held her breath.

"Will you agree to play another game of chess with me this evening?"

Having expected a very different question, this one took her by complete surprise. Augusta sat with her mouth slightly ajar trying to form an answer to his request. He wanted to play chess with her?

Augusta huffed out a breath but caught herself before saying something she would certainly regret. "Why yes, Lord Boxted. If there is no entertainment scheduled for the guests, I would be happy to meet you at the chessboard."

"Splendid." He smiled broadly. "It has been much too long since we played. I always relish a worthy adversary."

"As do I, my lord." She would endeavor to beat the gentleman in an even swifter manner than she had the first time they played.

"I say." He slowed the sleigh. "I believe that's my hat." The horse stopped and Lord Boxted thrust the reins into her hands. "Keep tension on them while I retrieve it."

Lips puckered, Augusta held the reins carefully as Lord Boxted waded through the drifts to grab the tall beaver, covered in snow.

The hat Augusta was determined to make him eat during the chess match tonight.

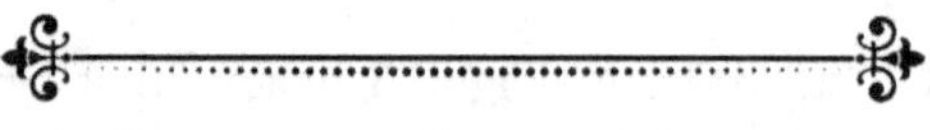

CHAPTER EIGHT

January 14, 1861
Welwyn Manor
Hertfordshire, England

CHRISTMAS HAD COME and gone with its excitement over his cousin Yule's engagement to Penelope St. Claire, giving Julius the perfect excuse to quit his London digs and return to his grandfather's estate. Ostensibly, the move was to lend support to his cousin in the days leading up to the wedding—something the entire family agreed Yule needed after their cousin Tom almost ruined the proceedings. A mere hiccup, according to Tom, but enough to make their grandfather call on all members of the wager to gather and make sure the wedding went off without a hitch.

This summons suited Julius royally. Appearing in Hertfordshire ahead of the festivities would allow him to continue wooing Lady Augusta. He'd not been able to see her at all during the holidays, so this seemed a God-given opportunity to continue his suit. When he'd discovered that Lord and Lady Tilney had been invited to the wedding and were in fact guests of his grandfather's, nothing could have pleased him more.

To this end, he'd inveigled his brother to travel to Hertfordshire with him for the express purpose not only of bucking up

Yule, but of helping Julius figure out the next step in his courtship. They'd scarcely left their parents' townhouse, where Francis still lived, when Julius pounced on his twin.

"Francis, I need your help with something."

His brother gave him a long-suffering look. "You are the one with the courtesy title, an estate in Norfolk, and the larger allowance, Jules. Why would you need my help?"

"Not with money." Julius stared out the window as the fashionable townhouses of Mayfair gave way to shops and various other businesses on their way to the train station. "With Lady Augusta."

His brother, riding in the backward facing seat, leaned forward excitedly. "You don't mean to tell me that you've gotten Lady Augusta to say yes?"

With a sigh, Julius sat back and shook his head. "No, not yet, although my hopes are high for the coming week at Grandfather's."

"Why?"

"Her family will be guests of Grandfather's for the wedding, so I'll have Lady Augusta close to hand." Julius shivered with anticipation. "I was this close, Francis," he held his index finger and thumb up with only a speck of distance between them, "at the Kastners' party. After we went for the sleigh ride, I think if I had proposed, she might actually have accepted me."

"Then why didn't you?" His twin sounded exasperated.

"Because I couldn't be positive her interests in me had changed." Although her reaction to their kiss had been most encouraging. The memory of those erotic moments in the sleigh always made him hard. "It was just a feeling I had and I wasn't about to bet the bank on a feeling."

"You have with every other wager you've ever made." Francis sounded grumpy. He'd lost many a wager to Julius's intuition.

"This was too important to leave up to a *feeling*."

"Never thought I'd hear you say that, brother." Francis raised his eyebrows. "But perhaps you are correct. The feeling about your chess game at the Kastners' was anything but accurate."

If looks could only kill, Julius would be a twin no longer. "Her king's knight came out of absolutely nowhere. I swear she'd hidden it somewhere and sprang it on me at the perfect moment."

"So that makes your tally two losses and two draws against her?" His brother grinned gleefully. "No wonder you don't want to trust your feelings. You really should arrange a rematch after the wedding. We'd all love to watch her beat the stuffing out of you again."

"Your entertainment is not my main concern at the moment." If he managed things correctly, he and Lady Augusta could make war over chessboards for the rest of their lives. "I have only one chance, Francis. One more proposal. If she doesn't accept me the next time, she never will. I have to make certain she understands the kind of man I am, the kind of husband I will be."

"Why would she think you would be anything other than the gentleman you have already shown her you are?" Truly puzzled, Francis frowned and cocked his head.

"The lady has reservations about the kind of life I must provide for her. Unlike so many young ladies who are quite literally champing at the bit to become a countess or marchioness, Lady Augusta has told me she eschews that kind of life. If given her choice, she'd marry a gentleman with no title or property who would allow her to roam the world with him."

His brother's face was agog with the news. "She told you that?"

"Not in those words, but the sentiment came across perfectly."

"And you never told me this before?" Francis looked more perturbed than Julius had expected. "Do you not suppose, brother, that this is the reason she refused you so many times?"

That brought Julius up short. Why had that never occurred to him?

"And makes your continued pursuit of her unwise." The concern on his brother's face was genuine. "I know you would not cause harm to the lady intentionally, Jules, but if you manage to persuade her to marry you against her own good judgment, would you not be doing you both a grave disservice?"

That very notion was the thorn in the plan for their life together. One he'd managed to push to the back of his mind in his mad pursuit of the woman he had come to love. Instead of redoubling his efforts, it now occurred to him he should withdraw entirely from his surreptitious courtship of Lady Augusta. Even if she agreed to marry him in the heat of a moment, like the one in the sleigh, would she not come to resent him when she had to eventually take up the official duties of countess? Would an all too brief happiness lead to inevitable dissatisfaction and utter misery?

He stared across the carriage at Francis, a wave of bleakness washing over him. "Have I been mistaken in my pursuit of the lady all along, Francis?"

His brother shifted uncomfortably. "If the lady has told you she does not desire the only kind of life you can offer her, Jules, do you even need to ask that question?"

Stunned, Jules sat staring out the window, seeing only Lady Augusta's beautiful face. How could he have been so blind as to let this happen? If he truly cared for her, he absolutely could not pursue her. His one consolation was that it would be his heart and not the lady's that would bear the brunt of his folly. If she had begun a nascent affection for him, it likely would pass away quickly. And if she did not, in the end, receive an offer from Mr. Burton, he was certain another gentleman existed who would be most willing to take Lady Augusta on the adventure of her dreams, without the encumbrance of a title.

The carriage rolled up to the train station and Julius descended, feeling as though the weight of the world had crashed onto his shoulders. In a daze, he headed for the first-class coach.

As though he understood his brother's turmoil, Francis saw

to the loading of their bags, then joined him in the train carriage. "Everything's taken care of, Jules."

"Thank you." Staring out the window at the grimy station walls, Julius sighed then closed his eyes against a world that was no longer kind. The coming week, one he'd so looked forward to, had just become a prospective hell on earth.

"WELL, YULE AND Penelope have reached London without incident." Francis entered the library at Welwyn Manor where Julius had retreated to brood about his decision to cease courting Lady Augusta.

Today had been especially hard for Julius. He'd had to sit and look happy while his cousin married the woman he loved more than anything in the world. Now that Julius had decided he shouldn't marry Lady Augusta, such a joyous event was no longer possible for him. All morning and afternoon, he'd managed to put a good face forward, even when he'd had to laugh and talk with Lady Augusta at the wedding breakfast. That had been excruciating, but Julius had excused himself as quickly as possible and hidden in the study with his cousins the rest of the afternoon. When they'd grown too rowdy, he'd retired to the library, believing his solitude secure there. Apparently, he'd been wrong.

"That is good news, brother, although I had no idea we feared for their safety. This is, after all, England during peacetime and the journey a matter of a couple of hours." Julius picked up the volume of Emerson's *The Conduct of Life* with which he'd attempted to lose himself after coming to the dismal decision not to propose to the lady again.

"Uncle Hugh expressed a doubt they would make the train in Digswell because they left so late." Francis sauntered in and took a seat in the soft brown leather chair opposite Julius. "You know how train schedules run, so there was some trepidation."

"Our cousin is on his wedding trip. He should not be held to a schedule." Julius propped his head on his hand and looked askance at his brother. "Besides, the station at Digswell is only three miles from here."

Francis shrugged. "You know how Uncle Hugh has always been about timetables."

Julius nodded, all too familiar with their uncle's foible. The man couldn't abide the idea of missing a train or ship to the point of obsession. He'd once made his entire family arrive at the train station half a day ahead of time in order to make absolutely certain they did not miss the train to London. Yule had told them this when they were boys and he and Francis had privately marveled that their uncle cared so deeply about such things. Their own father had shown such a lack of interest in punctuality that their mother eventually had to take over all travel arrangements whenever the family traveled together. "Then I'm certain Uncle Hugh is happy now. I've just never understood how he can get so worked up over a train schedule."

"Neither have I." Francis grinned and picked up Julius's book. "I mean, there will always be another train coming along if you miss the first one. What's this you're reading?"

"Ralph Waldo Emerson's book of essays." Julius slumped in his chair. "I was trying to clear my head."

Francis glanced at the tome and shook his head. "And this is the book to do that? I'd have thought Dickens or Trollope, perhaps would have fit the bill better." His brother peered more closely at him. "Are you still upset about your decision regarding Lady Augusta?"

"It's not something I took lightly, Francis." This was exactly why he'd been hiding in the library. He needed time and quiet in order to come to terms with this decision. "I'm very much in love with the lady and now I'm quite certain I'll never be able to marry her." He glared at his brother. "Do you have even an inkling how that feels?"

A smile played around Francis's mouth. "More than you might think, brother."

His brother's serious tone caught Julius's attention and he sat up, interested in something other than his own woes for the first time today. "What do you mean? Does this have to do with the mysterious lady you are secretly courting?" Until Francis had mentioned it in September, he'd not known his brother was interested in anyone. "You've said you have a lady in mind—but that's all you've said. Are you now telling me you've proposed to her and she's refused you?"

Francis sighed, sadness filling his face. "Yes, the lady I told you about before is the one I wish to marry." Francis got a faraway look in his eyes. "She is my rock and my strength when I am despondent. My best companion who never judges or faults me for anything. Quite simply she is the best person I have ever known, besides you, Jules."

Julius sat back, flabbergasted. "I had no idea, Francis. You've said not a word about her since… I still know nothing about her. What is her name? Who is her family?"

Francis paused, then shook his head. "I cannot say more of her. Not yet. I am trying my best, as you did with Lady Augusta, to persuade her to marry me—with as much success. I have managed to keep my life private, because we both wish it. So until she accepts me, I must keep her confidences and her name to myself. But I hope…I pray every day I can find the words to make her change her mind."

"What reason does she give for refusing you?" His brother might not have a title, still his character was unimpeachable and their family linage pristine. Francis was a very eligible *parti*.

Francis's face turned somber. "It is a matter having to do with her family. I cannot speak of it so I beg you not to ask." His pleading look went to Julius's heart. "I do not know what I shall do if by the time the wager is due, she has still not agreed to marry me, Julius." The agonized misery in his brother's face smote him, as Francis gripped his arm. "I cannot imagine living a single day of my life without her."

Julius patted his brother's arm, and sat back, sorely grieved by Francis's obvious distress. He was totally sympathetic to his brother's plight. At least Francis still lived in hope of persuading his lady to marry him, while Julius had to cease his attempts when he believed himself on the threshold of success with Lady Augusta. Fate was a cruel mistress, no doubt.

"Have you spoken to Lady Augusta?" Francis's voice was hesitant.

"Briefly, at the breakfast. She seemed eager to speak to me and I…I couldn't…" Julius had to stop a moment to get himself in hand. Lady Augusta's surprised expression when he excused himself after exchanging little more than "good afternoons" with each other was like a knife twisted in his heart.

"Perhaps you should find a way to tell her you are ceasing your pursuit." Francis suddenly seemed very interested in the dark-maroon leather covering his chair. "That might make it easier when you meet in public. To end things in a civil manner, so she won't be hurt or offended."

"She already believes I have ceased to court her, or at least, ceased to propose. Still…" That kiss might well have given her the idea that he was still interested in her. Which was true. And was why he'd done it. And if it was the only kiss they would ever share, he'd not be sorry he'd done it. But he should make it clear to her that he would not be renewing his addresses to her. "How can I do that without seeming cold or distant? I can't simply say, 'Lady Augusta, I will not be attempting to court you anymore.' Less than a month ago I told her I wanted us to be friends."

"Then what can you do to show her you part as friends?" Francis sat with his head leaning on his hand, brows furrowed in thought. "Some kindness?"

"Do you mean give her flowers?" That seemed rather mundane. Julius shook his head. "If I am going to part with Lady Augusta, I want her to at least remember me with fondness until she is a grand old lady. Some sort of grand gesture…"

A memory tugged at Julius's mind. "The cave."

"The cave?" Francis looked up confused, then realization hit him. "Oh, *that* cave." He cocked his head. "You want to take her to the cave?"

"The lady loves adventure." It was the perfect thing, the perfect place to say goodbye.

"Well, if that is true, then yes, I think it will do the trick." Francis rose. "I wish you luck, brother. When will you arrange the outing?"

"Tomorrow. Now the wedding is over I'm not sure how long Lord Tilney plans to linger." Oddly, Julius felt a lifting of his spirits. Whether it was because he would get to spend another morning with Lady Augusta or because he at last had a plan for what to do, he wasn't certain. But a calmness he'd not felt earlier had descended on him.

"Now that's settled, why don't you let me distract you for a little while? The cousins are getting up a game of billiards. Come play with us. Or just sit and take down all the wagers. That will cheer you up better than Emerson will."

"No thank you, brother. I think I'll stay here a while longer."

"Suit yourself, but you know where we'll be if you change your mind." Francis made his way to the door. "Don't let Emerson get the better of you."

"I won't." Julius sat back in the chair, and picked up his book.

A wave of his hand and Francis quit the room, pulling the door closed with a loud *click*.

With a sigh, Julius picked up Emerson and thumbed through the volume until he found his place again.

Whatever games are played with us, we must play no games with ourselves, but deal in our privacy with the last honesty and truth.

"Honesty and truth," he muttered. Those were the last things he wanted to admit. Because the honest truth was that he loved Lady Augusta, and likely always would. And because he did, he had to make the heartrending sacrifice of letting her go.

CHAPTER NINE

THE AFTER-DINNER ROUND of cigarettes and brandy that night seemed interminable to Julius. His grandfather's smoking room, decorated to resemble a cooling-room in a Turkish bath, was hazy with smoke, not unexpected as all the Quartermains indulged in their grandfather's store of fine Turkish tobacco. Tonight, however, the last thing Julius wanted was for the gentlemen to linger, talking about the wager, weddings, and when the next one of them would find a bride.

"So, who's next?" Alex took a long drag on his cigarette and sent a long tendril of smoke shooting upward. "Three down, three to go." He turned to Julius with a smirk. "Are you still wooing Lady Augusta? After your last drubbing from her at the chessboard, I'd have thought you'd leave well enough alone and seek another prospective bride. *Tempus fugit*, Jules."

It took all of his patience not to bark a retort at his cousin, but Julius refrained from engaging with him. The sooner they quit talking, the sooner they could join the ladies. "No, I'm not, Alex. I'm traveling to London with Mother when I quit here. She'd promised to introduce me around to some of her friends' daughters. I hope to have an announcement for the family by spring." That he managed to keep the misery out of his voice was a miracle.

"She led you a merry chase, Boxted." Grandfather came over

and draped an arm around his shoulders. "I'd hoped you'd have made a match of it. It would have been a solid alliance for the family and she seemed to suit you." His grandfather peered at him and Julius shrank back. "Are you certain you don't want to continue your attentions to her?"

"I'm afraid not, Grandfather." Julius had to find a way to make the torture stop. "I discovered that her affections lie with another gentleman. I have tried, as you know, to persuade her to transfer those affections to me, but she assures me her mind is quite fixed upon him. I will not disrespect the lady with further offers for her hand."

His grandfather gripped his shoulder in sympathy, then shook his head. "A shame, Boxted, but your instincts are correct. Mustn't devil the lady if she's made up her mind elsewhere." He released Julius and strode to the sideboard to refresh his glass. "Never fear. There are plenty of ladies who will be happy to bear the title of Lady Boxted."

Unfortunately, the only lady he wanted to marry did not.

Mercifully, the party broke up a quarter of an hour later, Julius being the first one out the door. He strode down the long corridor from the back of the house, where the smoking room had been relegated by his grandmother, who hated the smell of the tobacco, and at last entered the drawing room. He gazed all around the room, searching for the single lady he sought. At last his eyes hit upon her figure, standing at the window that overlooked the back lawn, gazing out into the darkness. With a sigh of relief at finding her to herself, Julius hurried toward her.

"Good evening, Lady Augusta." He bowed and waited for her to turn toward him, anticipating the moment he could look on her face once more.

"So you *are* speaking to me, Lord Boxted." The words were spoken with a hint of surprise wrapped in a cloak of sarcasm. "Had I wagered upon it, I fear I would have lost that bet."

Well, he'd known she'd been offended by his recent standoffish manner. "My lady, I beg your pardon. I have been remiss recently in not taking the time to converse with you. I pray you will forgive me, but I have been occupied with the preparations for Yule's wedding." That was a flat falsehood, but he hoped she didn't know that. The lie was better than telling her he'd been avoiding her. "But now the wedding is done, and I want very much to talk with you."

"Indeed, Lord Boxted." She turned to him at last, her face all frowns. "What could you wish to say to me?"

I love you and want to marry you with every fiber of my being. That's what he longed to say to her, but couldn't. "It's more of a question, really."

Lady Augusta straightened her shoulders and drew herself up to her full height. Her nose flared, her eyes snapped, and her chest jutted out, her magnificent breasts heaving with indignation. "What question could you possibly wish to ask me, my lord?"

"Would you please come out for a carriage ride with me tomorrow?"

As if his question had deflated her, Lady Augusta sank back on her heels, her shoulders now slumped. "What? Why do you want me to go driving with you?"

"Because I wish to spend time with you, my lady." The truth of that rang in his voice. "I have not had the opportunity to do so since we were at the Kastners' party, and I very much want to make amends for that." He looked at her with pleading eyes. "Will you come?"

She stared at him, her breath coming in little gasps as she thought about her answer. What he would do if she refused, he didn't know. Abandon the scheme, he supposed. But he so hoped she would agree. More than anything he wanted to give her this one little adventure before they parted company.

"Very well." There was still doubt in her face, but now that she'd agreed, he knew she wouldn't renege on him. "What time should I be ready? And where are we going?"

"I think after breakfast will be best." He gave her a sly look.

"As to our destination, that must remain a mystery for the time being. However, I do have one piece of advice for you."

"Pray there will be no stags tomorrow?" He so adored her wry wit.

"No." He grinned broadly at her. "Dress for adventure."

ONCE MORE AUGUSTA found herself wrapped well against the cold, waiting in the foyer for Lord Boxted. His cryptic advice to "dress for adventure" had intrigued her, although she had no idea what he was up to. Nor what exactly she should wear. There was no sort of adventure she could think of to be had in Hertford-shire.

There were no jungles to explore, no ruins to uncover, no river rapids to shoot. Well, there was the Mimram River that ran through the property. She'd seen it when they'd arrived for the wedding. But the river had looked broad, scarcely deep enough to float a boat, much less allow them to paddle down it. So the adventure Lord Boxted had alluded to must be of his own invention. Which actually made his request for her company all the more appealing to Augusta, once she put aside her pique at his strange behavior the past few days.

She'd hoped they would meet during the holidays—somehow she'd clung to his suggestion of going to London to see the pantomimes until she'd believed it was a *fait accompli*. But her parents had preferred to remain at home and Augusta had passed a quiet and dull Christmas, much as she always had. So when her mother had announced they were traveling to Welwyn Manor at the duke's request for the marriage of his grandson, she'd literally jumped for joy and danced around her bedchamber. Because she knew, without a doubt, Lord Boxted would be in attendance.

Much to her consternation, in the weeks since their thrilling sleigh ride—and that unexpected kiss—Augusta had thought constantly about Lord Boxted. Even though she'd always found him attentive as a suitor, she'd never seriously considered marrying him. She'd been convinced she would marry Mr. Burton and set out on a life of freedom and adventure. Absence was supposed to make the heart grow fonder, according to the poets, however her regard for Mr. Burton had seriously dwindled over the many months since she'd last heard from him.

Especially after her last meeting with Lord Boxted, who had shown his mettle admirably in bringing their sleighing adventure to a safe end. The gentleman's ready smile, easy conversation, and his long list of travels, while not as impressive as Mr. Burton's, certainly gave him the air of a debonair adventurer. Not to mention his excellent skill at chess coupled with his ability to take his losses to a lady with a grace not many gentlemen would possess.

All these considerations had come to the forefront when, just after the new year, her father had received a letter from Mr. Burton announcing his forthcoming marriage to Miss Isabelle Arundell. Father had sat her down in his study and ordered strong tea before he read the letter to her. Perhaps he'd expected hysterics from her, and rightly so considering how stridently she'd proclaimed she would marry Mr. Burton no matter what he and her mother had said. Instead, she'd had scarcely a twinge of regret, which she noted had puzzled her father immensely. She hadn't told him of the relief she'd felt upon hearing the news. Nor of her newfound regard for Lord Boxted. So she'd been excited to learn they were to journey to Welwyn Manor to the wedding.

But Lord Boxted had turned into an absolute boor toward her. When they'd met on the first evening, he'd scarcely spoken two words to her other than good evening. He'd avoided her after dinner as though she'd offended his closest relations, and had steadfastly refused to even look at her during the wedding or the breakfast. If she'd not had the company of her dearest friend Emma Bancroft, and her counsel not to ask Lord Boxted directly what was wrong with him, she'd have gone mad. Was there any wonder she'd been surly toward his lordship when he finally approached her last evening?

"Good morning, my lady."

She turned to find Lord Boxted, a charming smile on his lips, fastening his gray overcoat and looking more handsome than she'd ever seen him.

"Are you ready to set off on our expedition?"

Augusta pulled on her gloves. "That depends on where we are going. An expedition to the market in Welwyn will scarcely count as much as a daring trek across the Andes."

"You will have to wait a little longer for our destination to be revealed," he said, his eyes twinkling with mischief, "however I assure you it is neither the market nor the mountains."

"Very well, my lord. Lead the way." She declined his arm and marched out the door to the carriage, although she did allow him to assist her into it. Without hoops, she didn't want the long skirts of her riding habit to get caught on the carriage steps so she landed unceremoniously on the floorboards in front of his lordship. "I hope this outfit will suffice as adventure 'dress.' I have no idea what an adventurer wears in the wilds of Hertfordshire."

"Oh, you have chosen wisely, my lady. I believe your riding habit will suit the day's activity admirably." He tapped on the trap and the coachman opened it. "Drive on, Talbot."

Augusta gazed at him with narrowed eyes. "He knows where to go?"

"Yes, he does." Lord Boxted looked serenely out the window.

"And I am not to know?"

Smiling, Lord Boxted shook his head. "That would be telling, and I don't want to ruin the surprise." With that, he chuckled heartily.

Interest piqued in spite of her companion's glee, Augusta peered out the window at the wide fallow fields which quickly gave on to forested lands. The trees were thickly clustered, but as before in December, their leaves had left them spiky towers of black sunk into the pristine white snow. A landscape beautiful in its starkness.

Before long the carriage turned off the road and struck off to the right onto a faint pathway scarcely wide enough for a vehicle to navigate. Perhaps the adventure was beginning, although all Augusta could think was she hoped they did not get stuck in the snow and mud. The pathway wound through the trees toward a steep embankment that ran for some way in either direction. Curiosity rising, Augusta glanced at Lord Boxted who was smiling again.

"We're here."

The carriage pulled to a halt, seemingly in the middle of nowhere. The embankment before them seemed unremarkable, the grass and leaves covered in snow.

"Where is here?"

Lord Boxted opened the door, jumped down, then held out his hand to her. "The adventure begins."

Completely unsure what to think, or how to respond, Augusta put her hand in his, the warmth of him penetrating both his glove and hers. She stepped to the ground and gazed all around, confused as to why Lord Boxted believed a stroll in the snow and mud would constitute an adventure.

"Here you are, my lord." The coachman handed Lord Boxted two round glass-paned lanterns, the candles already lit.

"Thank you, Talbot." He took the lanterns, inspected them briefly, then handed one to Augusta. "Here. Follow me."

Amazed and amused, Augusta took the lantern and dutifully followed him toward the embankment. "Are you expecting an eclipse, my lord?"

Her turned back to her, his lips curled in amusement. "Not exactly. This way." He led her right up to the point where the land began to slope upward, then stood back peering at the thick leaves and vines covering the ground under the snow. Two more paces to the right and he handed his lantern to her, then reached forward, grasped the undergrowth, and parted it.

A slight rush of cold air brushed Augusta's face as a dark

opening appeared where Lord Boxted had moved the dead leaves, revealing a round opening in the earth, the edge ringed in stone.

Augusta gasped, her body trembling from excitement. "It's a cave?"

"Not just any cave, my lady. Here, hand me the lantern and let me go first." Lord Boxted took the light, holding it up near the top of the opening. "Give me your right hand and hold the lantern with your left."

She readily complied, trying to look everywhere at once. The smoothness of the stones suggested the rocks were not put there by nature. "Did the duke have this built? Or is it left over from an older mining operation?"

"Wrong on both counts." There was eagerness in Lord Boxted's voice. "But you are correct, it was built by someone." He walked slowly inside the cave and, trembling with excitement, Augusta followed.

The ground wasn't paved so she had to watch her step, but she trusted Lord Boxted implicitly. As they moved further into the cave, the outside light dimmed and they became dependent on the small circle illuminated by the lanterns. They revealed the sides of the cave were pockmarked here and there where stones had been dislodged, falling to the ground and making for treacherous footing.

Lord Boxted seemed sure-footed, however, and as the cave curved, he held his lantern higher, shedding more light into the cavern where the tunnel opened out. "This is what I wanted you to see, my lady."

Augusta held her lantern high as well, the small flame bringing into relief broken walls made of stone in the shape of a rectangle. A smooth section of stone seemed to rest atop the walls, although it was partially broken as well. She turned to Lord Boxted, her mouth agape. "What is this place?"

"As nearly as we have been able to find out, it is the ruins of a Roman bath house." Even in the flickering light, the excitement in his face was unmistakable.

"Roman ruins?" Heart beating so hard she had to gasp in air, August gazed back at the walls, imagining the ancient Romans who had inhabited Britain thousands of years ago standing where she now stood, going about their ordinary lives, getting ready to bathe. Awe filled her as never before. This *was* what it felt like to be an adventurer, to unearth something that no one had ever looked on before. Even though Lord Boxted obviously knew of it, still few people had stood where she was, looking at it. And now she was one of those few. Overwhelmed, Augusta had to simply concentrate on breathing.

When she could finally speak again, she asked, "How long have you known about this?"

"Oh, since I was a boy. Here, let's go this way." He led her forward, toward a smaller, round hole in the ground, also lined with stone. "Being brought to the baths was a rite of passage in the Quartermain family. About the time a boy reached the age of ten, Grandfather and some of the older family members would bring him out here and show him the ruins. He'd explain what they were, why the artifacts were important, and why it must be kept a secret."

"A secret?" Augusta looked back at him, frowning. "Why keep it secret? This find could be another Pompeii."

"For that very reason." Lord Boxted nodded. "I've been asking my grandfather to allow an archeologist to excavate these ruins completely ever since I was old enough to understand their importance. He does not want the site disturbed, doesn't want the Welwyn area to become overrun with all the people and machinery it would take to unearth the baths. Or the eyesore the area would become removing the tons and tons of earth it would take to bring the ruins to light."

"I suppose I understand that." Augusta gazed at the round hole, fascinated and frustrated at the same time. "It's a shame, however, that we can't know what these different areas were."

"The first area, the rectangle room is most likely the warm room. Romans had three rooms for bathing—a warm room, a hot room, and a cold room or bath." Lord Boxted moved them closer to the round area again. "This, I think, is the cold bath or pool, for cooling off after you came out of the hot bath." He raised his lantern again. "At the far end there is where they would have stoked a fire. Closest to that is a small room that would have been the hottest. The Romans sat there and steamed themselves. Then they moved into the warm pool to begin cooling down, then plunged into the cold water to finish their bath."

Augusta gazed up at him, awestruck. "How do you know all this?"

He shrugged. "I was curious, so I went to Bath and studied the baths there. Then I did extensive reading on the ancient Romans, especially anything on their architecture or on their baths." A satisfied smile curled Lord Boxted's lips. "My hope is that when my cousin, Lord Royden, inherits the dukedom, he will finally allow an excavation to begin. But until then, the family has a lovely little secret all to itself." He smiled at her, that joy on his face once more. "Don't you think so? I thought you would enjoy seeing it."

So much could hinge on the briefest moment of clarity.

Lord Boxted had known of these ruins for years, had visited them, studied them, knew them intimately. Yet the joy on his face when he first showed her the ruins was as though he was seeing them for the very first time. Because his pleasure wasn't in the ruins themselves this time, but in the joy it brought *her*. He truly understood what she desired in life and had managed to find a way to give it to her.

In that moment of perfect clarity, Augusta fell completely in love with Lord Boxted. It didn't matter that they were in the dark, they were cold, the air was dank, or the candles were flickering dangerously. All that mattered was that she loved him, wanted to be with him for the rest of her life. Who wouldn't wish to be with the man who would find a way to grant her wishes, even if they seemed impossible. Their life together would be the best adventure of all.

Suddenly, Augusta realized that she hadn't answered his question and the smile had begun to slip. "Oh, yes, my lord," she gushed, which she never did. "I cannot thank you enough for showing me a real archeological dig. This has quite been the adventure."

His smile returned, lighting up his face until her heart pounded like a hammer. She could stand and stare at him for the rest of eternity. But the chill was seeping through her shoes, and her shivers now were from cold rather than elation.

"Then I am a happy man, Lady Augusta." He gazed at her with such longing, she thought her heart would melt. "I wished to give you at least a taste of the adventure you seek." He sighed and glanced around the cavern. "We had best be getting back to the carriage. I tend to visit the ruins in the summer and it is cold here even then. The last thing I wish to do is give you a severe chill."

The heat Lord Boxted was generating through their clasped hands would keep some of the cold at bay, but he was correct. It was time to go, though she was loath to give up exploring the ruin. But she was comforted by the thought that they could return in the summer as he said, every summer or as often as they wished. She squeezed his hand. Once they were married they could find adventures whenever they chose. "Thank you, my lord. I do think that may be best."

The carriage ride home would be the perfect time for him to propose to her. After showing her how much he cared for her by bringing her here, the natural thing would be to ask her once more to marry him. She had been a fool to refuse him before, but she would not be so foolish now. As they picked their way back through the cavern and down the tunnel toward the light, Augusta could not remember ever being as happy as she was at this moment. She could imagine only one other that would exceed it—when she said "yes" to Lord Boxted.

CHAPTER TEN

THE CARRIAGE PULLED to a stop in the driveway before the sprawling Welwyn Manor house, but Augusta paid it no attention, was scarcely able to nod to Lord Boxted as he helped her down the steps. She kept her attention on smiling, on making certain Lord Boxted did not have an inkling of her distress when she spoke pleasantly to him as he escorted her into the house. "Thank you again my lord for the most thrilling morning of my life. I can't begin to tell you what it has meant to me."

If only she could tell him what she felt, what she wanted more than anything in the world. But she couldn't because he had not proposed to her. Far from it. He'd told her that he'd be going back to London with his mother in the next day or so as she wished to introduce several young ladies to him who would have their come outs in the spring.

Lord Boxted escorted her to the staircase. "I am so glad you enjoyed our adventure, Lady Augusta. I shall treasure it always."

"As will I, my lord. I shall never forget it." Her voice caught, and rather than have him hear her sob, she fled up the stairs.

She made it to the first landing before the tears began to trickle down her cheeks. What was she going to do? Blindly, she headed toward her chamber, but the thought of having to explain her current state to her maid was too much. Reversing her course, she started toward the opposite wing, making for the one person who might be able to help her.

Knocking loudly, she didn't wait for the "Come in" before pushing the door open to discover Emma lying in the large poster bed, her breakfast tray pushed to the side, sipping coffee. She bolted up off the pillows, the coffee sloshing over the rim and onto the coverlet. "Augusta! Don't you know better than to barge into a bedchamber without leave." Emma set the cup on the bedside table. "What would you have done had Alex been—My dear!" At last, her friend registered the tears that were streaming down her face. "What has happened?"

"Oh, Emma." Augusta flung herself down on the bed beside her friend. "I've lost him. I've truly lost him."

"Lost who, Augusta? Here, my dear, take this handkerchief before you drown." Emma snatched up the linen square from the table and handed it to her.

Augusta wiped her face, uncaring how blotched and red it might look. Nothing mattered now. "Lord Boxted."

"Lord Boxted?" Emma sounded terribly confused. "My dear, what has happened?" She leaned toward Augusta, putting a comforting hand on her shoulder. "Are you well? You look an absolute fright."

"I feel a fright as well. Oh, Emma." Augusta held the fresh linen to her face. "I've lost him. He doesn't want to marry me any longer."

"But I thought you didn't want to marry him." Her friend paused. "You refused him already, didn't you?"

"Yes, I did."

"Why?"

Augusta hung her head. "You know why. I was intent on marrying Mr. Burton. And I didn't want to marry a gentleman with a title."

"But now you've had a change of heart toward him?" Emma peered into her face. "That's all right, Augusta. You are allowed to change your mind about a gentleman." She withdrew her hand and Augusta sat up. "Can you tell me why you now wish to marry Lord Boxted?"

Tearing at the handkerchief, Augusta launched into the tale. "I wrote to you about the sleigh ride Lord Boxted took me on at the Kastner's party, didn't I?"

Emma nodded.

"What I didn't tell you is what happened after he saved us." Augusta started with that searing kiss, told her friend about Lord Boxted's aloof behavior toward her, and finished up with today's magnificent gesture and the aftermath on the carriage ride home. "His mother is going to matchmake him with some young lady who's not even out yet and there's nothing I can do about it." Tears began to trickle down her cheeks again. She'd thought she'd already spent them all. "What am I going to do, Emma?"

"What do you want to do, Augusta?" Her friend stared intently at her.

"I want to make him propose to me again." Only she had no idea how to do that.

Emma knit her brows together. "Are you willing to take drastic measures to convince him?"

"What do you mean by 'drastic'?" Augusta had to ask. Emma had married a man she'd known only four days. Her ideas about drastic might be too extreme even for Augusta. Of course, a lady could always arrange to get herself compromised as a path to the altar, but she'd never entertained such thoughts until now.

"What if instead of waiting for a proposal, you seduced him instead?"

Oh, yes, that was drastic all right. "I'd actually thought of doing that to encourage Mr. Burton, but I never got the chance."

"Well, you have that chance with Lord Boxted. Show him how you feel about him. Use your feminine wiles to make him desire you as much as you desire him." Her friend sat upright, an avid look on her face as she started to warm to her subject. "Most gentlemen would wish to see what kind of wife he will be taking to his bed on his wedding night." She shot Augusta a sly look. "A little preview of your delights may well tip the scales in your favor."

"Emma, for goodness' sake." Augusta's cheeks were hot. Even though she'd thought about seducing Mr. Burton, she had no knowledge whatsoever about what that would entail. Apparently, her friend could supply that lack.

She'd never known married ladies to speak this freely to an unmarried woman. Of course, all the married ladies she knew were her mother's age. She'd had few real friends growing up and she hadn't taken to her brother's wife when he married. Only Emma had gotten along well with her, likely because they were similar in many ways, yet different in others. So if her friend said she could help Augusta get Lord Boxted to marry her, she'd certainly listen to it. Even if it sounded mighty scandalous. "Is that what you did to get Alex to propose to you?"

"Not exactly." Her friend smiled a very knowing smile. "Alex and I were eager to marry for very different reasons. He, because of that family wager." Emma stopped abruptly. "You do know about the wager, don't you?"

"Oh, yes. I heard of it first when you did, after your wedding."

"And I wished for the security of his Regimentals." She stared steadily at Augusta. "You remember about my ordeal in India?"

Augusta nodded. "You told me when you married the captain, it was more for security than for love. I remember that." She glanced at Emma askance. "But you do love him now, don't you?"

"Terribly!" That smile was back, and broader than before. She blushed. "I think I fall more deeply in love with him each day."

"So you didn't have to seduce him." Augusta wished for another option as well. Being seductive wasn't something her governess had taught her in the schoolroom.

"No, but as soon as he proposed, we spent some very intimate moments on Lord Caxton's bower swing." Emma's cheeks deepened from delicate pink to fiery red. "With the result that the swing broke."

"Emma! That is *not* what you told me and Lady Caxton." Such antics were not anything Augusta felt herself capable of doing, not even to secure Lord Boxted as her husband. "Do I really need to do something like that?"

"Do you wish to marry Lord Boxted?" Emma's cool stare and pursed mouth spoke volumes.

"Yes."

"Then you need to do it." Emma shrugged her shoulders and stretched her arms. "It's not as though you won't enjoy it as well."

"Emma!" She wasn't so sure about that. She wasn't sure about any of this.

"Settle down and listen carefully." Emma leaned toward her. "If you want Lord Boxted to compromise you, the first thing you need to do is get him alone."

Fixing her mind on getting what she wanted, Augusta nodded. "How do I do that?"

"I'm certain you can arrange something." Emma waved her hand dismissively. "Gardens are ideal places for assignations, but as it's January, it's too cold out." She shook her head, her face filled with regret. "You won't get a rise out of him at all in this kind of weather."

"A rise?" Augusta was mystified.

"Don't worry about that. If you stay indoors, it should be fine." She sat back, thinking. "Libraries are good too. They usually have a key in the door, so you can lock yourself in with him. That way he can't bolt, and no one else can interrupt you. If I were you, I'd try for the library." Her friend peered at her. "You can do that?"

Determined, Augusta nodded. Emma seemed to have this seduction well in hand.

"Good. Get him in the library, lock the door, and hide the key."

"Where?"

Emma shrugged. "Some place Lord Boxted can't get it." She

raised one delicate eyebrow. "I'm certain you'll think of somewhere. Then, once you've gotten him alone, you need to kiss him."

"We did that already." Augusta could still recall the warmth of that kiss down to her toes. "But it didn't lead to another proposal."

Emma grasped her hands and held them tightly. "Do you want to marry him, Augusta?"

"Oh, yes. Absolutely."

"Good, because if kissing him didn't bring him to his knees in a proposal, you may actually have to seduce him into your bed." Emma's gaze didn't falter as she spoke those scandalous words.

Any other lady of Augusta's acquaintance would certainly have swooned. She merely gulped and nodded. "Then what must I do?"

"Well, once you have him in the library, kiss him again. Long and slow." Her friend settled back against the pillows, as though she was about to give a lecture. "If you're lucky, he will take over the kiss. Then matters will progress naturally enough. If he tries to deepen the kiss, open your lips at once, to allow him in." She smiled knowingly. "It's actually quite nice when you get used to it."

"Yes, it was." She'd have enjoyed the kiss more had she not been so shaken by the runaway sleigh ride.

"Oh, so he's done that already? Then he should take the lead again." Emma shook her head. "Men are never totally predictable, however. So if he doesn't take over the kiss, you must."

The whole business smacked of the more lurid romance novels the cook used to read in the kitchen. Augusta had purloined one and read it late at night, under the bed with a candle. She'd been thoroughly shocked but also thrilled by some of the things the ladies and gentlemen managed to do. "I won't know what to do!"

"Kissing is a good start." Emma patted her hand. "You liked it when you kissed him, didn't you?"

"Oh, yes. I did. Quite a lot."

"Good. Then you should put your arms around his neck and pull him to you."

"I did that." Augusta sat up eagerly, an idea occurring to her. "Perhaps I know more than I think I do."

"Some ladies know how to seduce gentlemen naturally."

Augusta hoped against hope she was one of those ladies.

"You can also tug on his earlobe with your teeth, like this." She demonstrated using her thumb and forefinger to pull gently on her earlobe. "I must say," she said, grinning broadly and giving her a saucy look, "that drives Alex absolutely wild."

Augusta's cheeks felt hotter than the kitchen stove. "I don't think you should be telling me all these things, Emma. It's not decent."

"Someone will have to tell you for your wedding night, if nothing else." Her friend looked at her skeptically. "Do you think your mother will give you all these details?"

"Never in a thousand years." Her mother still likely didn't know some of the things Emma was telling her.

"I didn't think so. Believe me, it's so much better to be pre-pared for…well, everything that happens on your wedding night. Although it may happen beforehand if you do a good job of seducing him." Emma leaned forward. "Do you want to know all about it?"

Even the little she'd done while kissing Lord Boxted had given Augusta stunning memories of the heat and strange flutterings that had flooded her body. If there was more of that to come, she wanted to know it. Surprises were very overrated. "Yes. Tell me all of it."

The next half an hour proved to be more of an education to Augusta than any information her governess had ever imparted to her about *anything*. Once her face had attained the heat of a small sun that could get no hotter, she settled down and forgot to be embarrassed. Emma had a way of explaining things so the actions and positions seemed natural, like learning which fork to use or which course came before another. By the time the clock on the mantle struck noon, Augusta had gained a wealth of knowledge about bed pleasures, as Emma called them. In a sense, she felt as though she'd already experienced more than many young brides did on their wedding nights.

"I'm amazed, Emma. Utterly amazed at this entire world unmarried ladies have no idea about." Augusta didn't quite know why older ladies kept this knowledge from the younger ones.

"At least you will not be ignorant on your wedding night, my dear." Emma giggled. "Or even on your next trip to a library."

"Let us hope the one will lead directly to the other." Augusta stretched, then slowly slid off the bed and onto the floor. "I don't know how to thank you. Goodness, I must fly. Luncheon will begin soon. Will you dress and join me downstairs?"

Emma lay back on her pillows, a dreamy look in her eyes. "No, I rather think I shall send a note to Alex to come here immediately. I am in need of his assistance."

"Are you ill?" Her friend didn't look indisposed at all.

"Not in the least." Emma's cheeks grew red for the first time. "My instructions to you have produced a powerful desire in me." She winked at Augusta. "Now it is my turn to try to get a rise out of my husband."

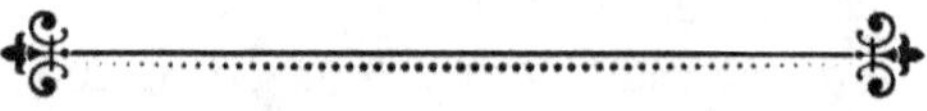

CHAPTER ELEVEN

GIVEN THE CHOICE of hiding out from his cousins in his grandfather's study or his library, Julius would choose the library every time. Not only was it more comforting—the bookish smell of hundreds of volumes, soft leather chairs that cradled you like a newborn, the blessed silence that encompassed one like a warm cloak—but the spirits kept there in the finest crystal decanter was only ever the best cognac his grandfather could find. Little wonder then that Julius had retreated to this sanctuary after saying goodbye, for all intents and purposes, to Lady Augusta.

He'd been more than delighted by her elation at their little adventure this morning. Nothing could have given him more pleasure than seeing her awe, her amazement at the ruins. Well, nothing save having her agree to marry him.

Julius sighed. If he could not give her the wonders of the world that she so desired, at least he'd given her this one brief happiness. Hopefully she would remember it, and him, fondly always.

Glass of brandy in hand, Julius perused the various volumes, looking for something to distract him from further thoughts of Lady Augusta, or worse the thought that tomorrow he must accompany his mother back to Town and begin the torture of trying to find a bride. If he weren't part of the marriage wager, he would likely leave that task for some years in the future. However, he couldn't let his cousins down, not when so much was riding on this wager. They all had to marry in order to win.

The library door clicked open.

"I'm still sure I do not wish to join you for billiards, Francis." His brother had importuned him to play not five minutes ago.

"Then I certainly won't attempt to persuade you to do so, my lord."

His head shot up, the spirits in his glass sloshed over the side as his gaze locked with Lady Augusta's dark-blue eyes. Julius's heart hammered in his chest. "What...what are you doing here, my lady?"

"I was...um...I was looking for Emma." She stood in front of the door, her back pressed against the dark panel, her deep-gold gown seeming to glow beside the darker wood.

"She's not...here." His mind had ceased to work clearly. "Perhaps you can find her upstairs." Much as he loved the sight of her, he knew instinctively that she should go. It had taken all his willpower to say goodbye to her earlier. Even though he was a man who prided himself on his self-control, at this moment he didn't trust himself to be alone with her.

"Yes, I suspect that is where she is." The lady continued to stare at him, not moving.

"Did you need...something...else?" The urge to grab her and wrap his arms around her had reached the point where his legs actually trembled with the desire to go to her and he had to physically stand his ground.

"Yes, I did." In one smooth motion, she turned to the door but instead of opening it, she seized the key in the lock and gave it a quick twist.

The click of the lock sounded like the snap of a trap being sprung.

"Lady Augusta, what are you doing?" Horrified, Julius stared as she held the key in her hand, gazing about as though looking for a place to put it. "My lady? What are you doing with that key?" Panic seized all of Julius's faculties. The two of them were literally locked in the room together. Alone. If anyone discovered them together like this...

Julius darted toward her, intent on grabbing the key.

Giving one more agonized glance around the room, Lady Augusta pulled the neckline of her bodice open and dropped the key down inside it.

Skidding to a stop directly in front of her, Julius gazed into her frank, determined eyes. "What the hell have you done?"

"I needed to talk to you, my lord. Without interruptions."

His gaze flitted down to her heaving bosom, imagining the key nestled there behind the layers of silk and cotton and boning. How bad would it be if he made a grab for it?

The idea of his hand fumbling between her breasts—her soft, white, perfectly round, previously untouched breasts—sent a shudder of lust tearing through his body. By the time he extracted the key, he'd no longer desire to leave the library.

He lifted his gaze back to her face just as she slid her hands around his neck and launched herself at his chest. Julius caught her as she pressed herself tightly to him, then her lips met his.

His first instinct was to protest this outrageous behavior, but that idea met a coward's death, swift and totally unsung. Instead, he slipped his hands behind her head, cradling it gently, luxuriating in the feel of her exquisitely soft hair, paired with her equally soft mouth, a touch that even now wreaked havoc in his breeches. Oh, but he'd dreamed of this moment for the past six months and by God he was going to enjoy it.

Pressing his lips to hers more urgently, he opened his mouth enough for his tongue to emerge and test the seam that sealed her lips. Was she desirous enough of him to grant him access once more?

Throughout their encounter, her hands had been busy stroking the short hairs at the nape of his neck, each caress more exciting than the last. When he pressed on her sealed lips however she gave a strangled squeal, then parted them immediately.

With a groan, Julius plunged his tongue into her willing mouth, sheer delight filling him at being allowed to possess that much of her once more. He withdrew only to thrust in again, exploring this very intimate part of her until she began to moan plaintively in the back of her throat. Good lord. This had to stop. He disengaged and thrust her from him. "We cannot do this, my lady. It's bad enough that we are here alone. If someone should come in—"

"They would have to break the door down to do it." Her chest was heaving, her glazed eyes dark as night. "I don't think they'll try it." She leaned toward him again, but he stopped her.

"Why are you doing this, my lady?" Julius couldn't fathom why she was behaving in this manner. "You cannot wish for me to compromise you. Then we will be forced to marry."

"I know." She reached up and cupped his cheek.

"But you have told me time and again you did not wish to marry me. That you did not wish for the only type of life I could give you." Staring into the beautiful face, flushed with obvious desire, he knew with absolute certainty that if he didn't find a way to leave this room immediately, he wouldn't able to stop himself from kissing her senseless. And God only knew what would happen after that.

"A lady is allowed to change her mind, isn't she, Julius?" The soft words, spoken with a plaintive note, wrenched his heart. Could what she said be true? The fact she'd used his given name, quite unexpectedly, lent credence to it.

"Then you would not mind eventually becoming the Countess of Winwick?" A spark of hope flamed up in his heart.

"If it meant I could marry you, I would become the Queen of England." She squeezed his hands. "Today you made me realize...I love you."

Julius ceased to breathe. Never had he thought to hear those words from her. "You do?"

"How could I not, after you found such an exceptional adventure just for me? Because you knew what it would mean to me." She ducked her head. "You are the epitome of the gentleman I have been looking for all my life."

"Not Mr. Burton?" He tried to peer into her face, but it was hidden from him.

"No, not Mr. Burton." She flung her head back, a tear trickling down her cheek. "You are far above that gentleman in every possible way." She sighed. "I am only sorry it has taken me this long to realize it."

Without hesitation, Julius seized her and crushed her against his chest. "Apology accepted."

She laughed and slipped her arms around him.

The simple motion made his groin ache. Everything she did, every word, every touch enflamed him as never before. He tilted her head up, her eyes shining as she gazed at him as though she'd found her hope of heaven. God knew he had.

Without pause he sank his mouth onto hers again, thrusting his tongue between her already parted lips, and reveling in the welcome he found there. Lost in her sweetness, he kissed her lips, moved to her cheek, strayed to her ear, his desire mounting all the while. "Do you want me to stop?" he whispered, his voice raspy now with his need for her.

"No." Panting, she frantically shook her head. Grabbing his hand, she tugged him toward the large leather sofa. "I want more."

Julius's eyes widened, even as he allowed himself to be propelled forward. Was this the proper Lady Augusta who had led him on such a chase? The woman would surprise him until he had one foot in the grave.

Suddenly, the great brown leather sofa loomed large beside them.

Lady Augusta stopped before the roaring fire, hot desire flickering in her eyes. "I want you to take me, Julius. Make me your own right this minute." Then with a plaintive tone, she added, "Please?"

Flushed and aroused as he was, Julius had to make certain she understood what she was asking. "Lady Augusta, do you know what you're saying?"

"I think if we are having this conversation, Julius, you understand you have my permission to call me Augusta." Her mouth puckered in a smile, but her steady gaze assured him she did indeed know what she was doing. "But to answer your question, yes I do. And I know I want you as I have wanted no other man before."

Heart beating frantically at a confession he never expected to hear, he gazed down into her beautiful, eager face and knew, as he'd known all along, this was the woman he loved beyond all reason. "I love you too, Augusta. More than anything in this world."

Tears sprang to her eyes. "Oh, Julius. I didn't think you would ever say that to me. Not when I've been such a fool."

"Shhh." He gathered her to him tenderly. "All that matters now is that we love one another." He kissed her ear, then continued to trail kisses down her neck, delighting in the shivers that wracked her body the lower he came to her decolletage.

Breathing in erratic little gasps, her whimpers grew louder with each brush of his lips. "Oh, Julius, I feel so…so strange."

"A good kind of strange, love?"

"Oh, yes." The low, guttural tone of her voice sent a renewed shiver of lust down to his groin.

Boldly, Julius ran his hands over her breasts, stroking them through the bodice he wished would magically disappear. What he wouldn't give to be able to tease her nipples into hard little points and then gently taste them. Well, that would have to wait for a later time. With heartfelt regret he removed his hands from her bodice. "Augusta, we should stop now. We can do nothing more here today."

"Oh, but I think you can, Julius." She stepped back and sat down on the sofa. Then sprawled back on it, her head pillowed on the arm, looking like a terrible wanton. "I think there is *much* more you can do."

"Augusta!" Shocked and aroused even more by the shameless display before him, Julius stared speechless at the luscious body lying before him. Her wide eyes glistened in the fire's light. "How do you know anything about what occurs between a man and a woman?"

A knowing smile spread across her face. "Emma told me."

"Told you what?" A suspicion dawned that his lady truly had learned more than she should have about the married state.

Her eyes beckoned to him. "Everything."

Julius caught his breath. If what Augusta said was true...if Emma had told her all about the most intimate acts of man and wife...dear God.

She reached her hand out to him. "Come show me, Julius."

"Show you...what exactly?"

"How you will make love to me." Stretching out fully on the sofa, she arched her back, thrusting her breasts toward him in blatant invitation.

Oh, damnation. Julius licked his lips and swallowed hard. After yearning for Augusta for so long, the temptation to do as she asked was almost impossible to refuse. They would be married shortly, in any case. No real harm done. And they'd certainly not be the first couple to anticipate their wedding night. Julius's cock strained against his trousers in full agreement.

Of course, the setting for this seduction wasn't ideal. They were in his grandfather's house with servants running all about, not to mention his cousins in a nearby room, some of whom might come in search of him at any moment. Still, he didn't wish to deny Augusta's passion for him, nor his for her. God, no. But the ultimate act of marital pleasures should be performed in a more private place, where no one could hear them.

So for now, he would give her as much pleasure as he could and let the other wait for another time. Say their wedding night.

"Very well, sweetheart." He moved to the sofa and knelt down beside her. "I will show you one way we can have marital congress and give you the greatest pleasure of your life. Will that satisfy you for now?"

"Oh, yes. I'm sure it will." She sighed with such longing, he wished it were possible to take her here and now. That moment, however, he wanted to be truly perfect.

"Here." He took her hand and laid it on his cheek. "Keep your hand here so you can feel me when I touch you." He peered into the deep blue eyes that did not waver. "You do know where I will touch you?"

"Yes, I do." She nodded, stroking his cheek and sending his desire licking through his whole body.

He certainly hoped she did know something about what he was going to do. He didn't want her to be frightened. Slowly, he slid his hand beneath her skirts and laid it on the smooth stockinged calf of her leg.

She drew a sharp breath but nodded. "It's all right. I trust you."

Skimming upward, Julius quickly reached the split in her pantalettes. Drawing the material aside, he slid his hand inside the garment, resting it against her thicket of curls. Her rapid breathing brought his attention back to Augusta's face, her eyes now round and wide as a startled deer—and staring straight at him.

He smiled encouragingly, and she cupped his cheek. So far so good. Not taking his gaze from her face, he began to stroke her mons lightly.

An array of emotions flitted across Augusta's face—surprise, shock, trepidation, wonder, and lastly, pleasure. He continued his gentle strokes, swirling his fingers all around her tender flesh. Her hips began to twitch, her eyes closed, and she began to pant and moan.

"Does that feel good, love?" he crooned to her as he brushed against the hidden nub of her pleasure center.

"Yes, oh, yes, Julius." Her hand dropped from his face and found his other hand, which she grasped and squeezed. "This feels so…"

"What, Augusta? What do you feel?"

"Wonderful." Her deepened voice had acquired a guttural tone that spoke of her need.

In response, Julius stroked more quickly, gazing at her face, watching eagerly as the tension in her body built.

"What…what is happening?" She clasped his hand in a frenzied grip. "Ahhh, Julius!" Her body arched as she shrieked, her hips bucked wildly, her face aglow with wonder.

"Shh, love. You're all right." Julius leaned over and kissed her trembling lips. Every part of her was trembling now. "Did you like that? Did it make you feel good inside?"

Flung back on the sofa, limp and panting still, she nodded. "I never felt anything that good before."

"I am glad to hear that, love." He slipped his hand from beneath her skirts, then helped her to sit up on the sofa.

"Must I get up? I'm so very tired." Her lids were scarcely open and she looked as though she would curl up in a ball if he took his arm from around her.

"In future, we will remain in bed afterwards, but we are not in bed now nor in a very secure place." Julius gave her a wink. "You can give me the key now, my dear." At last he'd managed to put her in check, a feat he'd not been able to do often at the chessboard. He rose and pulled her to her feet, then dropped a fleeting kiss on her lips. "I think no one will be the wiser to our téte-à-téte if you go quickly upstairs to your room."

She busied herself pulling the key out of her bodice. But as she handed it to him, she gave him a meaningful glance. "Just think, Julius, two adventures in one day. And I am hard put to say if I enjoyed our forbidden interlude here more than our visit to the ruins." She swayed closer to him. "Perhaps I need another adventure like this last one to help me decide."

"My love, we will have plenty such adventures once we are married." He smiled as he rearranged a curl that had become dislodged during their interlude.

"But this secret interlude has been especially thrilling because of the risk of discovery." She gave him an arch look. "Couldn't you arrange another one for tomorrow?" There was a wheedling tone in her voice now. "One that would continue what we did today?"

"Augusta." She had that look on her face he'd come to know all too well. The one like a horse with the bit in its teeth.

"You can arrange it, can't you, Julius?" Her eyes were liquid blue pools. "So we can share everything between us?"

She wore that pleading look again—the one he'd have to get used to giving in to. He'd wanted their wedding night to be special, but perhaps, knowing his bride, an "adventure" would be more special to her. But where could they meet for this sort of tryst with no one the wiser? An inn was too public and too common. The ruins would be dark, cold, and uncomfortable, although he could see the appeal that might have for Augusta. What else was nearby yet remote and somewhat rustic? A glimmer of an idea occurred, and he smiled. "Very well, my dear. I'll meet you in the foyer to go riding tomorrow afternoon. Can you arrange that?"

Eagerly, she nodded. "Emma said a secret rendezvous was the most fun of all."

Julius chuckled. He might have to speak with his cousin Alex about his wife telling tales out of school. "But I assure you, my love, Emma was right."

CHAPTER TWELVE

THE THIN AFTERNOON sun threw shadows on the ground as Julius and Augusta rode through the densely wooded tract of land two miles south of Welwyn Manor. A brisk wind whistled through the surrounding trees, most denuded of their splendid fall foliage. They were extremely fortunate there'd been no snow since Christmas to further impede them, otherwise Julius wouldn't have been able to arrange this tryst, an event he was very much looking forward to.

The idea of finally having Augusta in his bed had taken some time to sink into his brain after they finally left the library yesterday afternoon. Once it had, however, he seemed to be able to think of nothing else. Dinner had been spent sending surreptitious glances at Augusta across the table, increasing his desire to have her to himself tenfold. Unfortunately, their after-dinner conversation in the drawing room had been forced to remain mundane as they'd not been able to speak to one another alone the entire time.

First, he'd had to inform his mother that they could not leave for London as scheduled. And as he couldn't tell her what was transpiring between him and Augusta, he invented a wager with his cousins to explain why their departure must be delayed. That was always the easiest excuse for people to believe when it involved a Quartermain.

Of course, then he had to actually propose the wager to his cousins and brother. Knowing his mother, she might well ask to be in on the wager herself, which meant there had to be one. He'd have to be canny in the timing of things, but he believed it would work out in the end.

The result had been that he and Augusta exchanged longing looks surreptitiously all evening and by the time he climbed into bed that night, all he could imagine was the morrow's tryst, with visions of Augusta sprawled naked across the bed, her long hair brushing against the smooth creamy skin of her breasts, her nipples pert and peaked, ready for him to taste. Such images had led to a quick and not completely satisfying eruption. But at least it had relieved the tension and allowed him to sleep soundly so today he could make Augusta irrevocably his before proposing to her for the very last time.

"Can you please tell me where you're taking me, Julius?" Augusta's plaintive question had been asked several times since they'd met in the foyer.

"It's not much further, love. Are you cold?"

"No." She sent him a sly glance. "Excited."

Her husky tone sent a shiver of desire down Julius's spine, fueling his imagination once more. Images of their tryst to come were so vivid, his cock sprang to life, making its demands all too apparent. Gritting his teeth, he urged his horse into a trot.

Less than five minutes later, they emerged into the clearing surrounding the rustic cabin his grandfather had often used as a hunting retreat in his younger years. Julius and his brother and cousins had made up hunting parties when they'd been youngish gentlemen, but as Grandfather had aged, the cabin had fallen out of favor and into disuse. No one used it these days save for occasionally Uncle Hugh, Yule's father. With a very slight possibility of discovery, Julius believed he could safely press it into service of a different sort today.

They came to a halt and Julius quickly dismounted, tied up their horses, then turned back to assist Augusta.

Laughing, she slid down into his arms, her blue velvet riding habit accentuating her perfect figure as his hands held her trim waist.

She grasped his head and pressed a delicious kiss on his lips before turning toward the path to the cabin.

"You go ahead in. I'll stable the horses and be in directly."

She nodded, the jaunty black feather atop the little blue hat perched on her head bobbing in agreement.

With one hungry look at her retreating figure, Julius pulled on the horses' reins and led them around back to the stable. By the time he'd joined Augusta in the main room of the cabin, he could scarcely contain his excitement at the prospect of the pleasure they were both about to experience for the first time together.

Peering out the window, Augusta sighed, then turned to him, a concerned line wrinkling her brow. "You're certain no one will come to this cabin while we are here? There's still some hunting going on, according to my father."

"No, I swear to you, this retreat is scarcely ever used any-more." He sidled up behind her, slipped his arms around her, and drew her back against him. "We will be quite alone, I promise you."

"But it doesn't look as though it's fallen into disuse at all. The rooms look as though they've been recently refreshed." There was an edge of panic in her voice that he needed to banish.

"That is because I came out here early this morning and tidied it up." He nuzzled her neck. "I wanted this to be as comfortable and exciting for you as possible. Another type of adventure all together."

She turned in his arms and laid her head on his shoulder. "This is why I changed my mind, Julius."

"What do you mean?"

"I told you long ago that I wanted a life quite unlike my mother's, unlike that of most young ladies my age. I wanted the freedom to do things most of society would frown on or be shocked at. A life few men would be willing to give me." She looked up at him, love shining in her face. "You proved to me you were one of the rare few who would make my life one adventure after another." Grinning, she stood on tiptoe and pressed a kiss to his lips. "Like whisking me off to the woods to have your way with me."

He bent his head to her ear. "Shall I have my way with you now, sweetheart?"

She stared hungrily into his eyes. "Yes, oh, yes, my love."

With a swift motion that drew a shriek of surprise from her, Julius swooped her up in his arms. "As I think I have said before, your wish is my command, my lady."

He stalked over to the cabin's main bedroom, carried her over the threshold, then kicked the door shut.

⟫⟫⟫✕⟪⟪⟪

SQUEALING WITH SURPRISE and excitement, Augusta clung to Julius's neck as he strode into the bedroom, cradled in his strong arms. The room was spacious and clean, with a warm fire crackling in the fireplace, what looked to be thick, new covers on the bed, and a small rough-hewn table that held a variety of fruits and cheeses and a bottle of wine.

Julius kicked the door shut, then spun them around the room until her hat flew off, and she was laughing and dizzy. "Julius, stop. Stop before I am unwell."

He slowed to a halt, then carefully set her on her feet. She wobbled a bit, and he steadied her, brushing a stray wisp of hair off her forehead. Lord knew what her hair looked like after that spin. Better than it would by the time they'd finished here, for certain.

That thought sobered Augusta but only for a moment as Julius's mouth descended onto hers. The dizziness returned as she could scarcely breathe for the pounding of her heart. Immediately he sought entrance to her mouth, and she opened oh so willingly, reveling in his intimate caress. Boldly he explored her, his tongue stroking hers, then darting here and there, creating a longing in her for more of his attentions.

As though he could read her thoughts, he slipped his hands upward until he cupped her breasts. Even through layers of clothing and whalebone, his touch lit a flame deep inside her. Moaning in anticipation of everything yet to come, Augusta pushed against his hands, trying to feel more of his touch and becoming frustrated when she could not.

Julius broke the kiss, his eyes normally so intense a blue, now black and filled with an undisguised hunger.

Her stomach twisted at the sight of that raw desire, her body responding with a throbbing sensation deep at her core.

"Let me help you with your clothing, sweetheart."

Augusta nodded and, biting her lip quickly undid the long row of buttons down the front of the jacket. A wave of cool air touched her skin and she shivered as he quickly stripped the garment from her. She rubbed her arms where the icy air had made gooseflesh rise all over her. The chill was replaced immediately by a surge of heat as Julius set his lips to the nape of her neck, at the same time slipping his hand around to cup her breasts.

"Oh, Julius." Eyes closed, she couldn't move for the flood of sensation that overpowered her. The trail of kisses down her neck made her arch her back like a cat, luxuriating in each slow movement of his mouth.

Suddenly, her corset loosened, and he drew it off her, letting it fall to the floor. His hands covered her breasts, stroking them softy through the thin layer of her linen chemise until her nipples stiffened into tight little peaks and her breasts swelled. Never had anything felt so good as when his fingers caressed those hard points. Each time he brushed them, it sparked a delicious coiling down in her nether regions.

Reveling in these strange new sensations, Augusta stood still, trying to savor everything happening at once. Every movement he made incited new flutterings inside, as he untied the her skirt, letting it fall to a heap on the floor. He then finished removing her chemise, drawing it slowly over her head, leaving her naked and exposed to his devouring gaze. Suddenly aware as never before of her completely unclothed state, Augusta tried to turn away from his hot gaze. However, he stopped her, and turned her back toward him.

"You must allow me to feast on the sight of your perfect body, my love." His eyes roved over her, taking her in from head to toe, approval in his hungry gaze. "You are the most beautiful woman I have ever beheld, Augusta." He seemed unable to take his eyes off her. "I knew it from the moment we met, but I couldn't have imagined just how exquisite you would be until this very moment."

He drew her to him and kissed her mouth, slipping his tongue inside so naturally, she was scarcely surprised. Then it was gone as he continued his caresses down her neck, across her chest, dipping into the cleft between her breasts before making a trail down to the tip of her nipple. He circled it with his tongue once, then clamped his lips around the entire tip.

Knees buckling, August gave a cry and grabbed his neck. Suddenly she was scooped into his arms and carried swiftly to the bed, where he laid her gently on the coverlet, shivering with a raging desire that crashed over her in a tidal wave.

"Let me disrobe, love, then I will join you." He doffed his jacket then began to swiftly strip off his clothing.

Her breath coming a little steadier now, Augusta crawled under the covers, all the while not taking her eyes off the fascinating display as Julius removed piece after piece of his clothing, revealing more and more of the sleek body she'd only ever imagined. Except for Greek statues in the British Museum, she'd never seen a naked man before, so now she was about to find out for herself if the Greeks had gotten it right.

Down to his shirt, breeches, and boots, Julius looked over at her and raised an eyebrow, as if seeking approval. There was still a lot left to her imagination, but not for long, so she nodded and dragged the covers up to her neck. He pulled off his Hessians, then slid the stockings from his legs, revealing well-shaped calf muscles. She must have made some sort of noise, for he glanced back up at her, gave her a wicked grin, and unbuttoned his breeches.

Augusta swallowed convulsively as he peeled them off. There was a flash of bare skin, a glimpse of his huge member jutting out that was immediately hidden by the voluminous folds of his shirt. Eyes wide, forcing herself to breathe, Augusta watched as he stalked toward the bed then sat beside her.

"You're not frightened are you, love?" He spoke soothingly as he stroked her cheek.

"A little." Emma had explained about a man's member, but Augusta had thought her friend had perhaps held back somewhat on her description of the size of it. Or else Julius was simply bigger than other men.

"That's to be expected." He kissed her softly. "Do you want me to continue? We don't have to do this now. We can wait until we are married, you know."

Augusta shook back her head. This was what she wanted. "We will have all our married lives to do this, but just this one chance to be scandalous. We can't anticipate the wedding night after the wedding."

Chuckling, Julius rose. "In that you are correct, my love." With one fluid motion he pulled the shirt over his head and tossed it to the floor, now towering over her in all his naked glory.

Oh, yes. The Greeks had certainly gotten it right. Julius did indeed rival Adonis. The broad shoulders, the sculptured chest, the stomach rippling with taut muscles, right down to the strong arms and thighs and slim hips. The only thing they'd not depicted correctly was the huge member that jutted straight out at her. Augusta's breath seemed to leave her body in a single whoosh.

Still, she had to admit he was everything a woman could ever desire. And he was about to be hers for the rest of her life.

He drew back the covers and she slid over to make room for him. The bed was small, but that didn't matter. They were going to be very close no matter what.

Julius slipped beneath the sheet and gathered her to him, pressing his bare skin to the whole length of her body. "We'll warm up in a minute."

"I suspect so." Suddenly nervous, Augusta couldn't stop trembling. She understood well what was about to happen. Emma had been quite clear on the details—her friend was remarkably frank for a woman in Polite Society.

"It will hurt, you know." He tucked a tendril of hair back behind her ear.

"I know." Her friend had spoken plainly about that, in particular. "But only for a moment or two."

"You do know quite a lot about this, don't you?" He turned toward her, slipping his hands over her breasts, cupping them firmly.

"Yes." The word came out in a gasp. How could it be otherwise when he was stroking and caressing her bare nipples like that? Was he trying to distract her from the next thing to come?

And suddenly Julius rose over top of her, straddling her body, his hot heaviness unexpected, yet exciting. With a gleam in his eyes, he slid down and lowered his mouth to her breast, then engulfed the nipple once more, sucking on it gently.

"Ah, ah." The sensation was like nothing she'd ever known before. As he drew in again, that coiling sensation down at her core sprang to life, growing more intense each time he pulled on her flesh. The coil began to spiral upward, just as it had done yesterday, leading to that amazing burst of pleasure. If that was where this was leading, she was oh so ready to oblige.

Julius shifted his body and his hand brushed her curls, causing the spiraling to quicken each time his hand and mouth worked together, pushing her toward the top…

Instinctively, she lifted her hips against his hand, pressing it hard against the nub and suddenly she was soaring, shattering, bursting from within as waves and waves of that most intense pleasure shot through her body. Panting as though she'd just run a race, Augusta slumped against the mattress, well spent and more than content once more.

"You enjoyed that didn't you, sweetheart?" Julius whispered in her ear.

"So much." She hugged him to her. "It's the most incredible feeling. I don't know why women must wait until marriage to experience it." She peered up at him. "Men obviously don't."

He chuckled. "Well, you didn't either."

"I am an exception." She snuggled down against him once more.

"You certainly are exceptional." He kissed her neck. "Which is why I love you so very much." He shifted up over top of her once more and peered down at her. "Are you ready?"

"Yes." This must be the actual thing this time. She certainly hoped she was ready for this.

"Just relax and I will take care of you." He slid his body down until he covered hers. "Open your legs, love."

Steeling herself, Augusta did as he asked. Immediately a hot, hard pressure appeared at her entrance.

"Raise your knees...yes, that's it." Julius pressed his rigid member right up against her opening.

Closing her eyes, Augusta gritted her teeth, tensing against the pain to come.

And it did come.

With a grunt, Julius thrust forward. There was a great deal of pressure, a sharp stab of pain—like a cut from a sharp knife— followed by a stinging, burning sensation as he continued on, filling her up to the brim with himself.

Unable to help herself, Augusta cried out, more from surprise than from the pain itself. And to her horror, her eyes filled with tears.

"Augusta!" Julius froze, his face a mask of fear. "Did I hurt you that badly?" The agony in his voice made her tears flow faster. "Are you all right?"

"Yes, I'm fine." But the wretched tears wouldn't stop trickling from her eyes, running down the side of her face onto the pillow. "I'm quite all right. Just terribly surprised by the…feeling…of you." As if this wasn't already going all wrong, her cheeks began to burn with the embarrassment of having to explain all this to him.

"I hurt you that badly?" He stilled himself, his face quite pale. "We should stop. This can't be right if you're hurting this much."

"It's not the hurt." She simply didn't have the words to describe what she felt. "The first pain is gone. It was only like a cut, not truly bad. Now it just feels…strange. I don't know why I'm crying." She wiped at her tears with the back of her hand, praying they would subside. "Truly, I'm fine. Please, don't make us stop."

He peered down at her, a brooding look on his face.

A horrible thought occurred to Augusta. "Unless…this is all there is to…it?"

With a groan, Julius hung his head. "You will be the death of me, Augusta Hardy." He raised his head to look at her. "No, that is not all there is to making love. You should know that by now."

"What do you mean?"

"What just happened…and what happened yesterday?"

Her eyes widened. "That is supposed to happen now too?"

"Yes, but for the both of us." He frowned. "Did your friend forget to tell you that part?"

"Perhaps I didn't listen so carefully after a while." There had been so much to consider during Emma's talk and some of the things she'd said had distracted Augusta more than she'd like to admit. "Can we continue, or do we have to start all over?"

Julius closed his eyes and growled low in his throat, which then turned to a chuckle. "Just lie back, sweetheart and let me take care of everything."

Nodding, Augusta tried to relax back on the bed, happy to let

Julius take over. She obviously didn't remember as much of Emma's talk as she'd thought she did. "I'm ready."

He lowered his mouth and dropped a blistering kiss on her lips, then thrust forward, filling her again, more fully than last time. The strange feeling of fullness was still there, but the pain didn't return. That was a blessing.

When he began to pull himself out of her she was puzzled and disappointed, because he'd just said that—

Oh! He lunged back inside her, the sensation beginning to feel more normal. There was even a pattern, a rhythm beginning to form. Glide forward, pull back. Forward and back. And if she lifted her hips at just the right time, his body brushed against her little pleasure nub. "Oh, Julius, that feels so good."

The coiling sensation had begun again.

"God, yes, it does, sweetheart." He smiled down at her. "You have no idea."

"Yes, I do. Oh, yes!" He'd brushed the nub with his hand, sending her spiraling upward. Before she reached that peak, however, he sped up his thrusts, pumping into her time and again. He touched her nub again and Augusta cried out as she shattered around him, exploding with pleasure as her body gripped his over and over again.

Julius thrust into her once more, then cried out her name and suddenly she was filled with liquid heat. He slumped over her, but rolled to the side before he could crush her. They lay side by side, Julius panting as though he'd had an apoplexy.

Alarmed, Augusta dragged herself up to peer down at him. "Are you all right?" She shook his shoulder. "Are you dying? What is going on, Julius?"

Still gasping for breath, Julius shook his head and pulled her down on top of him. "I'm… fine. Have to…catch my breath."

Greatly relieved, Augusta relaxed into the warmth of him. "Thank goodness. I wished I'd known more about…everything that happens."

"You know more than most young ladies do now." He

wrapped his arms around her and she could hear the racing *thump thump* of his heart.

"I can only think how shocked they will be on their wedding nights." Her own would now be much less frightening. "At least I know what to expect from now on."

Julius chuckled. "My love, we have only scratched the surface of how a man and a woman can pleasure one another. And we will discover them all together, one after the other, as soon as we are married." Now that sounded most interesting indeed. Emma had hinted that there wasn't just one way a husband and wife enjoyed marital congress, as she'd called it. And if they had to wait for marriage in order to do this again, well that could take months. Her brother's engagement had lasted almost seven months. Having discovered the amazing feelings of pleasure Julius could give her, she had no intention of waiting so long to experience them again.

He raised his head to stare intently down into her eyes. "You will marry me now, won't you? If not, we are both in for a lot of explanations should you now be carrying my child."

Running her hand across his broad chest, Augusta gave him a sly smile. "Why don't we meet here tomorrow afternoon and I will give you my answer—after you show me more ways we can give one another these pleasures?"

"Augusta, you cannot be serious." Julius sat up, bringing her up to sit beside him. "You must agree to marry me."

"Come here tomorrow and you'll receive your answer." She reached up and grabbed his earlobe between her teeth, then gently pulled downward.

Julius shuddered. "Where did you learn to do that?"

She grinned triumphantly at him. "I'll tell you my secrets after you show me yours—tomorrow."

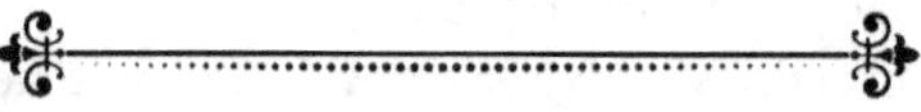

CHAPTER THIRTEEN

NEXT MORNING, AFTER another interview with his mother reneging on their journey to London, which she took with less grace than before, Julius hurried to the foyer. The time he'd appointed for him to meet Augusta was fast approaching and he didn't wish to be late. He asked a footman to have his and Lady Augusta's horses brought around, but Warner, the family's butler for generations, appeared with Julius's hat and stopped him. "I beg pardon, my lord, but Lady Augusta has already gone out."

"She did what?" Julius hoped the shock didn't sound quite so strong in his voice as he feared it did.

"Yes, my lord. The lady said she was meeting you at the assigned place and when you showed up here, to tell you the plan had not changed." The butler blinked, but otherwise did not comment.

"When did she leave?" And more importantly, "Did she ride out alone?" Aghast at the thought of such a thing, Julius snatched his hat from the butler and prepared to run out to mount Brutus and take off after her. The land around Hertfordshire was usually quiet, however young ladies did not ride unaccompanied. There was always the fear of being accosted by some vagrant or unscrupulous gentleman, although knowing Augusta, he rather thought to fear for the person who might try to accost her.

"She left around an hour ago, milord, and took Bobby the

second groom with her."

Julius stopped and sent up a prayer of thanks for that, then managed to breathe again. "Thank goodness." He turned to the footman. "Fetch my horse now. I cannot keep the lady waiting." Julius strode outside, then paced like a madman until Brutus arrived, mounted and started off at a canter. He was supposed to have met Augusta in the foyer at ten. Why she would take it into her head to leave so early and without waiting for him was puzzling. Had something upset her? Replaying their conversations of last night, to see if he'd said or done something to give a reason for this change of plan, bore no fruit whatsoever. Of course, the lady was capricious and had a mind of her own, so anything was possible.

He urged Brutus on toward the cabin, wondering how Augusta was going to explain her destination to the groom. The servant accompanied her specifically to make certain no such assignations could take place, so even if she paid the lad handsomely, he would end up talking to someone in the kitchen and eventually it would make its way upstairs. Then Lady Augusta's reputation would be in shreds. Well, they would be married shortly, so perhaps the scandal wouldn't be quite so dire. He shook his head. His future wife seemed to be enjoying their illicit trysts far too much to want to give them up. It was a problem he would need to deal with, and soon.

At least scandal would ensure not only that she married him, but that she did so without a lengthy engagement. Now that he'd had Augusta in his bed, he didn't see how he could spend another night without her soft, voluptuous body pressed familiarly against his. Or how his cock would manage without its snug nest. Lord, he could scarcely wait to show her some of the other things ladies were not supposed to be aware of before their marriage.

Just imagining the first of those things made his cock harden until he had to pull the horse down to a walk and wait until he'd gotten himself under control. From his body's reaction to the mere thought of Augusta, he feared they would see little on their wedding trip save the inside of their hotel room. He saw nothing wrong with that. However, as Augusta hadn't been to any city outside of England, she would likely object to a schedule of lovemaking that didn't include at least some time to sightsee and shop.

As Julius neared the cabin, he began to wonder what Augusta had done about the groom. He certainly hoped she hadn't tied him up along the way. That might sound farfetched, however knowing Augusta as he did, he wouldn't put it past her. Another scandal in the making that would lead to inquiries that would certainly ruin her reputation quicker than a telltale servant. Julius sighed and touched his heel to Brutus's side, urging the horse to greater speed.

The clearing around the cabin was quiet, no sign of Augusta, her horse, or the groom. A strange foreboding came over Julius. Had Augusta decided, for some unknown reason, against their tryst and actually gone for a ride? Considering she was supposed to give him her answer about marrying him today, her absence would be a dire signal that she'd suddenly had another change of heart and no longer wished to marry him. And if by chance she'd been caught with child yesterday, well then there would be hell to pay for sure.

Julius rode Brutus around back to the stable, dismounted and walked the horse into the old wooden structure. An interested nicker greeted him and Brutus, and Julius sighed in relief.

Augusta was here.

He quickly stabled his horse next to hers and hurried back around to the front door of the cabin. He opened the door, looking around eagerly. "Augusta?"

There was no sound, save the crackling of the fire he'd come over and lit earlier this morning when he'd tidied the bedroom, preparing for their rendezvous. He had to admit, these clandestine meetings, tinged with the excitement of possible discovery had heightened both his pleasure yesterday and his expectation of today's tryst. Augusta had been right about that. He'd have to find a way to persuade her that the threat of discovery could be every bit as real when they were married. They'd just have to make love in places where they might be found in very compromising positions.

"Augusta?" A glance told him she wasn't in the main chamber. He scanned the corridor leading to the rest of the cabin and spied the door of the master bedchamber, where they'd frolicked yesterday, slightly ajar.

Invitingly ajar.

Heart beat pounding in his chest, his groin tightening in anticipation, Julius pushed the door open.

The fire snapped and popped merrily in the grate, illuminating the room with a gentle glow that revealed Augusta, lying in the bed, the covers pulled up as far as her breasts, which jutted toward him, two perfect, creamy globes, the dark nipples furled into hard nubs from the chill in the air. Her eyes were pinned to him, a rueful pucker to her lips. "Well, you took your time getting here, Julius. I was beginning to think I'd need to find another way to keep myself warm."

Dear God.

The sight of her naked body coupled with the deep, throaty purr of her voice and the intense, raw desire in her eyes sent a surge of lust so powerful through Julius, his cock sprang forward against his breeches hard enough to make him grunt. Without a second thought, he tore at his clothes, his only thought that he must possess that luscious body immediately, before he spilled himself here and now. The stubborn material didn't wish to cooperate, so a few buttons went flying as he ripped them from his trousers, but in less time than he'd imagined, he stood over the bed, naked and panting, and snatched the rest of the bed-clothes off her.

Augusta gave a little squeak of surprise but didn't move a muscle.

His breath stopped at the sight of her curvaceous, creamy white skin, a treasure just lying there ready to be plundered. With a low growl, Julius dove into the bed and crawled slowly toward her.

Augusta's gaze never left his face, though she did giggle nervously the closer he got, until he covered her, dipping his head and clamping his mouth over one of her dark nipples, groaning at the delightful taste of her.

Her hands came up to cradle his head, pressing it to her breast as she moaned low in her throat, her legs shifting restlessly underneath him. After a moment, she guided his mouth to her other breast, her cries growing louder as he sucked her nipple, taking every ounce of control not to explode. When her groans reached a fever pitch, Augusta opened her legs wide. "Take me now, Julius," she panted in his ear. "I can't wait any longer for you."

Needing no further urging, Julius hurriedly positioned himself at her opening, guided himself just inside her, then gave a mighty thrust, crying out with the joy of homecoming as he slid snugly all the way to the hilt.

"Oh, Julius." Augusta clutched at him, seeming to want to touch every part of him at once. "It feels so marvelous." She strained against him, as if seeking to draw him even deeper within her.

"Wait, love." He was so close to the edge he needed to stop, before he spoiled it for her. "I need a moment." He panted, trying to hold still, to think of something other than the tight sheath that surrounded his member. "I need to slow down…to breathe."

But it was no use. The rapturous look she gave him, her eyes begging him to continue completely undid his resolve. He snaked his hand down between them until it rested at the apex of her thighs, in the nest of delightful curls, and murmured, "We'll do this better next time."

"Next time? But this time isn't—Oh, oh, Julius!"

Massaging her little nub, Julius began to move within her, unable to stop himself from withdrawing and thrusting home again and again. He tried his best to bring her with him to the pinnacle and just as he began to spill himself, her body clenched around him.

"Oh, oh, yes. There, there." Almost begging, Augusta pushed against him as he cried out, emptying his essence deep inside her warm sheath as it gripped and released him over and over until he fell away from her, completely and joyously spent.

Augusta lay beside him, staring up at the ceiling, gulping in air every bit as frantically as he did. She turned to gaze at him, a smile spreading over her face. "What were you saying about next time?"

He chuckled still panting though his heart had ceased to race like a thoroughbred. No other woman had ever affected him as Augusta did, in bed or out of it. His life from now on would be very different with her as his wife. If only she would agree to be his wife. Although after yesterday and today, he didn't know how she could put off the inevitable engagement any longer. It was dangerous for her reputation and his.

Because now she had him, like a fish on a hook. Having ruined her, he could not as an honorable man marry anyone else, even if he wished to do so. But if it became known that he'd ruined her and hadn't made provisions to marry her, he'd be considered dishonorable as well. No matter how long she drew this out, he would have to play along.

Well, they would see about that.

Perhaps keeping her satisfied was the best way to bring her to the altar. She'd enjoyed yesterday's lovemaking so much, she'd extorted him into today's meeting. If she wanted him to act as teacher, then he'd begin another lesson now. "While we are here and so wonderfully situated, I thought I could show you some more adventuresome ways a man and woman can have amorous congress."

"What do you mean?" She rolled over so her breasts rubbed very pleasantly against his chest.

"Well, one thing is the different positions we can use. It doesn't have to happen only with you underneath me." Gazing into her beautiful face, sweaty with their exertions, Julius once more felt his cock stir. The woman herself acted as a powerful aphrodisiac to him.

Her eyes glittered with interest. "What kinds of positions?"

"One you might enjoy is called 'Riding St. George.'"

"What is that?" She rolled over so she lay directly on top of him.

"Almost what you are doing now." He grinned up at her. "St. George rode the dragon if you remember. And now you are going to ride me."

Her eyes widened and the excitement in her face gave him gooseflesh. "Show me."

With the foreboding that he might be slipping the leash of a dangerous tiger, Julius lay back on the pillow and grasped her hand. "First you'll have to pique my interest."

She cocked her head and frowned until he guided her hand down to where his member already flew at half-staff.

"Now, grasp me—not too tightly or you'll hurt me." He winced at her enthusiastic grip. "Loose enough that you can stroke me up and down easily." Demonstrating, he wrapped her hand around him, then drew her lax fingers upward.

Her eyes had grown wide again, her irises a blue ship in a sea of white, but thankfully she wasn't squeamish about taking hold of him, and ran her fingertips lightly all the way to the tip. "Like this?"

"A bit tighter…yes, that's right." With a contented sigh, Julius settled back, eager to see what she would do next, and amused by the serious concentration on her face. She was absolutely adorable, determined to get a rise out of him—and in the best way possible. "That's good, sweetheart." Better than good. He was already fully erect. "Now you can release me."

"Why?" She sounded more than a little disappointed.

"Because it's time for you to mount the dragon."

"Oh!" The surprise on her face was delightful.

"Just like you're riding a horse astride."

For the first time a shadow of doubt crossed her lovely face.

Well, he wasn't about to give this up now. Raising his eyebrows in an unmistakable challenge, he grinned as her brows dropped into a vee.

"Very well." She climbed atop him, her nether regions pressed to his stomach, her legs on either side of him. "Like this?"

"Almost," he groaned, the intimate touch of her so intoxicating he felt giddy. He grasped her waist and lifted her up. "Guide me in."

The flash of naughtiness that shot across her face acted as another potent aphrodisiac. Julius's cock stiffened miraculously as she slid him into position, her lips grasping him as he slowly lowered her onto his fully erect member.

The look of awe that came over her face was erotic beyond belief. Every move the woman made set him aflame. Her tight sheath grasped him so snugly, he was again afraid of spilling himself too fast. At last, Augusta sat astride him, with his cock fully inside her. Absolute heaven.

"What do I do now?" she asked, leaning forward to whisper in his ear.

Groaning in pleasure, Julius almost forgot to control himself. She felt so damned good, he could scarcely think of anything else. "Exactly what you're doing, love. Lean forward and act as though I'm your prize stallion."

"You *are* my prize stallion." She laughed and stroked his face, then began to do exactly what he'd requested, starting slowly, then picking up a quicker pace. "Shall we take a jump?"

Julius had no idea what she meant, but he grasped her hands and pulled her closer to him, thrusting upward in counterpoint to her movements again and again.

A look of wonder came over Augusta's face, half pleasure, half awe as her body began to clasp him. "Oh, Julius. Yes, yes!" She threw her head back, calling out as she shattered around him.

"Oh, God. Augusta." Julius thrust one last time, a moment that seemed to last an eternity, as he spent himself deep within her soft folds. For one unforgettable moment, he thought he would never stop, his climax lasting longer than ever before. Utterly exhausted, panting so hard he thought his lungs would burst, he clasped Augusta to his chest, his body going limp into the mattress. "I think…" He really couldn't speak for panting. "I think you may have killed me, my love. I'm done in." His heart was still thudding against his chest. He wouldn't be surprised if she could feel it. "I cannot feel my body because it's floating somewhere out there." He made a feeble gesture toward the ceiling.

She chuckled and burrowed her face into his shoulder. "You had better come back down. We have something important to discuss."

Julius shook his head. "No. The cardinal rule of perfect amorous congress is that you cannot discuss anything serious for at least an hour afterward." He winked at her. "No man is able to say no to a woman who has just satisfied him to the fullest."

"Not even to discuss their engagement?" She peered into his face, one delicate eyebrow quirked upward.

Julius thanked God and slumped against the mattress. "If you give me just a few minutes, my love, I will be more than happy to discuss our nuptials." He smiled at her and grasped her hand. "I have waited so long to hear you say yes."

"But I haven't said it yet, have I, my love?" She squeezed his hand excitedly. "I'm not certain I want to say yes quite yet." Raising his hand, she looked into his astonished eyes as she kissed it. "We have had such wonderful adventures here, I want them to continue on, at least a day or two longer. The possibility of being discovered is quite thrilling."

"Augusta! You promised to answer me today." For all he sounded shocked, it was no more than he'd expected. The lady wanted to have things her way. Well, she was going to get it. "If you don't promise to marry me this minute, I will turn you over and spank your bottom."

Her eyes grew round and wife, her mouth a huge O. "You wouldn't dare."

"I wouldn't?" He dove over on top of her as she shrieked and tried to roll out of the bed. He grasped her around the waist and hauled her back, turning her over so her bottom faced up. Running his hand over the beautiful round globes, he asked, "Will you answer me or not?"

Before Augusta could answer, the thunderous noise of a great many horses coming into the clearing in front of the cabin froze both of them.

"Who is that?" Augusta whispered vehemently, her head coming up, her face stricken.

"I'll look." Julus grabbed up a blanket that had slid onto the floor and pulled it around his hips. He glanced at her, struggling to get under the sheets. "You'd better dress as quickly as you can. Do you need help?"

She shook her head, then threw off the covers and made a dive for her clothes laid across a chair in the corner. "Who is it?"

Julius padded to the window and peered out between the curtains. He muttered a curse. "It's Uncle Hugh and a party of gentleman. From the look of them, they've come here to shoot." He swallowed hard. "Your father is with them."

Augusta uttered a strangled cry and leapt for the garments, making them cascade to the floor. She grabbed the blue riding habit and undergarments and began frantically pulling them on with a quickness Julius would not have believed. "What are they doing here? I though you said no one comes here anymore."

"Uncle Hugh is about the only one of us Quartermains who still does."

"But isn't hunting season over?" She'd managed to pull on her undergarments save for the corset. Taking a good look at it, she tossed it into a closet. "I can do without that." She then proceeded to step into the habit's full skirt.

"Pheasant is in season until the end of February." Julius pulled up his breeches, wishing frantically that he still possessed all his buttons. "I suppose this is his last hurrah for the season."

"It's going to be the end of us, Julius." Buttoning her bodice, Augusta took a moment to send him one tormented look, then went back to working on the long line of buttons, not very tidy but mostly holding the garment together.

"I doubt that, my dear, although it will certainly be the end of our courtship." Julius stuffed his shirt unceremoniously into his waistband, then pulled on his boots and grabbed his jacket. "Do you mind terribly?"

She gave him a withering look then opened the bedroom door, Julius following closely behind her.

The cabin's main room was crowded with huntsmen, his Uncle Hugh and Lord Tilney standing in the middle of the floor, arms crossed, identical looks of reproach on their faces.

Augusta stopped so suddenly Julius almost bumped into her. His gaze flickered from one man to the other, wondering which one of them would speak first. The lady opened her mouth as though she would explain, then apparently thought better of it and closed it again.

At last Lord Tilney spoke a single sentence. "I assume this means that when we return to London, our parish rector will begin calling the banns."

Julius leaned forward until his lips met Augusta's ear. "Checkmate, my dear."

She gave Julius a long hard look, then nodded before turning back to her father. "No, Papa, that is *not* what is going to happen. Tomorrow Lord Boxted is traveling to London, to visit the Archbishop of Canterbury and secure a special license. Then, as soon as we return to London, Lord Boxted and I will be married at once." Throwing back her shoulders, Augusta swept out of the cabin, head held high, without a backward look.

Julius hurried after his betrothed but stopped beside Lord Tilney. "Thank you, my lord. Your presence has thankfully hurried along the inevitable marriage."

The glint in Lord Tilbury's eye made Julius's blood run cold. "You'd best see to it that it does, Boxted."

Julius bowed and all but ran after Augusta. He might not have needed his future father-in-law's assistance, but as with anything having to do with Augusta, better safe than sorry.

CHAPTER FOURTEEN

London
February 1, 1861

AWASH WITH SUNLIGHT and laughter, the Tilneys' London townhouse seemed to Julius the perfect setting for his and Augusta's wedding breakfast. Now that the ceremony at St. George's was over, he could hopefully relax and enjoy his wedding day.

Of course, Julius had never been prouder or humbler than when Augusta had stared lovingly into his face and repeated her vows without a single hesitation. The look of pure joy in her expression made his heart stutter so violently, he almost couldn't repeat his own vows. He'd heard the phrase "my cup runneth over" but not until that moment had he truly understood it. Today he was by far the luckiest man alive.

"What are you daydreaming about, my love?" Augusta cocked her head, a mischievous look on her face. "Or do I truly need to ask?" The saucy look she gave him set him to thinking about the coming night with Augusta in his bed beside him—or underneath him—all night long. No, he'd best *not* think of that, else he'd tent his trousers.

The past two weeks had been incredibly long, as he and Augusta had been forbidden to be alone together ever since being discovered *en dishabille* in Grandfather's cabin. He only hoped Augusta never found out that he'd suggested to Uncle Hugh that a final hunting party of the season would be just the way to finished off Yule's wedding festivities. Nor that he'd suggested her father might enjoy being part of the party. Not that Julius believed Lord Tilney enjoyed finding his daughter and her lover all but in the throes, still the ultimate goal—today's nuptial celebration—had been worth the recriminations and the scoldings from their families, and the black looks he'd gotten from Augusta. Those had lasted only until he'd stolen a few moments on the ride back to Grandfather's to stop the horses and kiss her senseless. A long conversation had ensued as they walked the horses home, in which he'd suggested a speedy marriage would afford them all the time in the world to play as they had in the cabin. After that she quieted down and plans for their marriage proceeded apace.

Sadly, that stolen kiss was the only intimacy they'd been able to snatch for the past two weeks as the plans for the wedding had gone forward. After producing the special license as promised, Julius had been summoned back to Grandfather's house in Norfolk and kept there cooling his heels, pining for Augusta until yesterday when he'd been allowed to rejoin the crowd in London—with Francis as his watchdog. That was now all in the past. He and Augusta were married and about to embark on a lifetime together.

"No, my love, I don't think you need to ask at all. Because I suspect it is what you have been thinking about as well." Julius took her hand and kissed the palm, letting his mouth linger there.

"I have been thinking that it's almost time to cut the cake, Julius." She laughed and drew her hand away, slowly. "Somehow I doubt that is what you were thinking just now."

Before he could answer that, Emma came running up to them, her cheeks quite pink. "Augusta, you must come. The bridesmaids want to begin their games and you must be there." She glanced at Julius and grinned. "No husbands allowed, I regret to say, Julius."

"You may steal her away only for a moment, my dear." He gave his bride a searing look. "We have unfinished business to attend to."

"I'm sure you do, my lord. Come, Augusta." Emma grabbed her hand and tugged her toward the doorway to the main receiving room.

"Good afternoon, ladies." Francis approached just as the two headed out the door. "I say, old chap. Someone's run off with your bride if I'm not mistaken."

"Quite all right, Francis." Julius's gaze lingered on Augusta's retreating figure. "I know where to find her." He clamped his hand onto his brother's shoulder. "My grateful thanks again for standing as best man."

Francis shrugged. "What are twin brothers for, if not that? I just wanted to say congratulations again." He lifted the glass of champagne he was holding. "You managed to pull off a feat to rival Alex's marriage less than ten days after meeting Emma."

"What do you mean?" Julius pulled out his pocket watch. He and Augusta had to leave in plenty of time to catch their ship that would sail at six o'clock this evening. It was only half-past two now, but he couldn't wait to be completely alone with his wife for the first time in a very long fortnight.

"No one would have wagered you'd end up married to Lady Augusta, Jules. Not after she refused you time after time." Francis shook his head, a smile playing over his lips. "We were beginning to wager on how many times you would propose before throwing in the sponge."

"And who was keeping the book on these bets?" Julius wasn't certain whether to be more indignant over the wager or about another cousin taking over his duty with the book. "I certainly wasn't."

"Tom."

"God." Julius shuddered. "That must have been a right mess." He gave his brother a hard stare. "How many times did you put down?"

Francis grinned. "Eight. I know you better than the others, you see. I knew you'd continue until she married somebody."

"And eight seemed a good choice to you?" Julius didn't know whether to be peeved or amused.

"Eight's my lucky number." Francis gave him a sly look and downed his drink. "We were born on the eighth of October, we have eight in our immediate family, and I was born eight minutes after you. Thank you." He set his glass down as a footman passed by with a tray of empty glasses. "Or so Father claims."

"Why do you deem that lucky?" Julius had always wondered why his twin wasn't more jealous, considering that eight minutes had cost him a title, position, and wealth.

"Because then I would have been named Julius, and that would have been too much of a cross to bear." Francis ducked as Julius swung at him.

"I may be an old married man, Francis, but I can still thrash your arse any day of the week."

The two sparred playfully until their mother hurried over.

"I should not need to tell you two to stop this behavior at once. And on your wedding day, Julius." Mother gave them her sternest look—that melted into an embrace of her eldest son. "You need to find Augusta and head over to the cake table, my dear." She tried to detach Francis's arm from around Julius's shoulder.

"Not just yet, Mother." Francis took Julius's arm. "The cousins want a word with him as his tenacity regarding Augusta has cost several of them hefty sums."

"Wagers." Their mother threw up her hands. As a Quartermain herself, she understood all too well how fruitless it would be to argue with them about anything regarding wagers.

Francis propelled his brother toward the rear of the house, to the library of all places. Well, he thanked God for the libraries he'd inhabited recently.

A quick knock and the door opened on the gathered cousins—all save Yule. He and Penelope had offered to return for the wedding, but Julius wouldn't hear of it. A wedding trip happened once in a couple's lifetime and he wanted his cousin to enjoy his to the hilt. All the others, however, turned toward him as Francis ushered him in and shut the door.

"Congratulations, cousin." Alex came forward with a glass of brandy in his hand and offered it to Julius. "Thank you, by the way, for making me a much wealthier man today."

"Happy to oblige as always, Alex." Julius took a huge mouthful of spirits. He could have used it earlier as he stared at the altar, waiting for Augusta to appear and praying that she would. The woman would keep him on his toes, no doubt. He supposed he needed to become accustomed to uncertainty ruling his life.

"I'd never have wagered so heavily, Jules, had anyone told me Emma was thick as thieves with Lady Augusta." Tom's bitter tone was offset by his good-natured grin. He turned a sour look on Alex. "I cry no fair, cousin. You had inside information."

"To be honest, even Emma didn't know if Augusta was going to actually accept him." Alex tried to hide his smile behind his glass. "Of course, once she told me the advice she gave her friend about seducing Jules, I suspected the die had been cast."

"I wasn't sure she was going to marry me until she was standing at the altar this morning saying, 'I will.'" Julius spoke up, provoking laughter from all present.

"So are you finally convinced, cousin?" Sandy leaned against the library table, a smile playing around his mouth. "Or do you think she will bolt yet?"

"Well, my plan is to keep her so busy she won't have time to plot an escape." That was Julius's actual plan once they could be alone. When they arrived in their first destination, Venice, they would see little of the city for a good week if he had his way.

"Busy shopping and sightseeing, or busy in your bed?" Tom's lecherous grin gave no doubt which option he'd choose.

"Both, although I'll try to persuade her toward the latter option." Julius shot him a knowing look. "And I think I'll be the winner of that argument." They both would. "So now it's Francis's turn to come up to scratch. Or yours." He fixed his cousin with a steely eye. "The rest of us haven't done our duty just to have you two slackers ruin it for us all."

"I still have seven whole months to find a bride to marry. Don't rush me, Jules." Tom strode over to the sideboard and poured himself another brandy.

"So that leaves you to be next in line, Francis." Julius turned to his brother with a smirk. "I hope you can now tell us more about the mysterious lady you are fixed on. And let us know when you have named the day. Seven months may sound like a long time, but *tempus fugit*. Look how long it's taken me."

"All in good time, Jules." Francis looked up from the snifter he'd been staring into. "I can't tell you more until I convince her to marry me."

"Where did you meet her, Francis? And when?" Sandy spoke up from the chair he'd been occupying. "I didn't know you'd been attending entertainments this past fall."

"I attended some." Francis was beginning to sound defensive. "Suffice it to say I found her, even though I've had some other things on my plate," he gazed around the room, pointing to Alex, Sandy, and his twin, "including all of your weddings plus Yule's."

Sandy looked about to speak up, but Francis cut him off. "No, I didn't attend your actual wedding, Sandy, but I was certainly there for the one where you were jilted." He stared them all down. "Jules can tell you I have been going out to the usual social engagements—balls, musical evenings, card parties. I have been doing my duty, and I have found the lady. Just give me leave to convince her to marry me."

"Well, if you take after your twin and take six months to convince her, you're going to be cutting it close to get it done by August." Alex nursed his drink, dismayed. "Can anyone think of any way to speed the process?"

"House party." Tom raised his head from the depths of his snifter. "That's how you met and convinced Emma, you recall."

He grinned. "Then we can all be there to help you with your wooing."

"That's not a bad idea." Sandy leaned forward, his face suddenly alert. "Who has a house available for a weekend party?"

"Grandfather, of course." Julius had picked up Sandy's excitement. "The home of a duke is the perfect place to introduce her to the family. The wives can be most encouraging." He'd love to help his twin secure the woman he so wished to marry. "Although if you plan to hold it before the end of April I'm afraid Augusta and I won't be there. We aren't supposed to return to England until then."

"Emma and I can come and be of moral support," Alex spoke up quickly.

"And Isabelle and I, although…" Sandy hesitated, his cheeks turning pink. "I doubt we'll be out in company by April." He looked sheepish. "I seem to have put a bun in the oven already."

Amid cries of congratulations, Alex's face turned red as well. "Dash it. Emma won't be out in company then either."

"I thought she looked fuller than usual. Congratulations, to you too, Alex." Julius grinned at his cousin, now hell bent on bringing Augusta back from the wedding trip in the family way as well. Couldn't let his cousins out strip him, could he?

"I guess I'll have to be the one to assist Francis in bringing his true love up to scratch." Grinning broadly, Tom raised his glass high. "You're welcome."

Francis groaned. "I believe I will not require assistance from any of you, thank you all the same." He bit his lip, suddenly pensive. "A house party does, perhaps, sound like a good idea as a way for me to introduce the lady to everyone…and pray God after that she'll even consider marrying me." He glanced around the room. "If we held it in early March do you think you could all manage to attend? You must know something about convincing a lady to marry you. All of you seem to have done so—with devastating speed."

The others laughed and Julius slapped his brother on the

shoulder. "We all found love in the blink of an eye, didn't we?"

"You didn't take much time to decide, although you took the longest to accomplish it so far, Jules." Francis's smile didn't quite reach his eyes.

There was a discreet knock at the door of the library, and Emma appeared. "Augusta is looking for you, Julius. She says it's time to cut the cakes."

Julius set his glass down on the desk so hard, the contents sloshed over the rim and cascaded into his hand. "Tell her I'm coming now please, Emma."

She nodded, blew a quick kiss to her husband, then left, closing the door.

"So you're at Augusta's beck and call already, Jules?" Tom snickered and rolled his eyes.

Shaking his head, Julius headed for the door. "I've been at her beck and call almost since I met her, Tom." He sent his cousin a smirk. "And I wouldn't have it any other way."

Quitting the library, Julius hurried to the large receiving room where the multiple tiered white cake, decorated with tiny flowers of pink icing, towered over the two-layer chocolate groom's cake. "Here I am, sweetheart."

"I didn't think I'd have to send out a search party on our wedding day, Julius." Augusta gave him a rueful look. "Am I going to have to chain myself to you for the duration of the wedding trip?"

"I can think of worse things you could do," he whispered in her ear as he took his place beside her. With a glance around the room, he began boxing the pieces of cake Augusta had already cut for the guests to take home with them.

His wife blushed to the roots of her dark hair. The cake knife in her hand wobbled, cutting off a sliver of cake instead of the usual substantial sized piece. "Here, my lord. Make yourself useful and dispose of this please." She lifted the bit toward him and, eager for a morsel of anything to eat, Julius dutifully opened his mouth.

At the last moment, however, she turned her hand so the sliver of cake ended up plastered to his lower lip and chin. She stood giggling at him. "Oh, Julius, I'm *so* sorry."

He narrowed his eyes at her as he scraped pieces of cake and icing off his chin and popped them into his mouth. "Think nothing of it, sweetheart. It's actually very tasty."

"Is it?" She gazed at him with merry eyes.

"Oh, yes." Julius grabbed one of the slices she'd already cut. "You should try it too." Without hesitation, he pushed the piece of cake into her mouth, catching it partly open, so some of the confection did get in. A good bit of it, however, landed all over her chin.

"Julius!" Her indignant tone was far outstripped by her laughter as she scrambled to wipe the icing off her face and put it into his mouth.

To his surprise, when both cake and her fingers met his tongue, he instinctively sucked on them, staring lustfully into her widened eyes.

Slowly, she withdrew her fingers, then plastered her mouth onto his, her tongue immediately thrusting. A surge of heat shot straight to his groin and he pulled her to him, unmindful of the cake or the crowd of people who were gathering around them.

When he finally broke the kiss, panting, he glanced around to find all eyes on them.

Augusta ducked her head, but not before he saw the desire clear as day in her eyes—a look he'd sorely missed these last two weeks.

"Ladies and gentlemen, we seem to have had a mishap with the wedding cake." He took his bride's hand and led her from behind the table. "We must go tidy-up, but we will return to continue cutting your slices."

"Where are we going?" she whispered.

"Up to your bedchamber. There should be soap, water, and towels there." He cut his gaze toward her. "And a bed, I believe."

Her eyes widened.

"Does it also have a lock?"

She nodded.

"Excellent." He started them down the corridor toward the staircase. "I know just the place to hide a key."

⇒⇒⇒✦⇐⇐⇐

FRANCIS CHUCKLED AT the spectacle of his twin and Augusta slathering cake all over one another's faces. Much as it surprised him, he had to admit Augusta was the perfect wife for his brother. They seemed to be evenly matched in temperament, in intellect, in their desire for out of the ordinary adventures. The only place Augusta might outstrip Julius was at the chessboard. He'd be interested to see if their games became more evenly matched over time. Jules had always been a quick learner, if he didn't get distracted. Francis certainly wouldn't wager on that one.

His brother gave his new wife a searing kiss, then quickly swept her from the room. Well, Francis suspected they would not be seen again for at least an hour—he certainly hoped they wouldn't miss their ship. He also hoped to take this opportunity to steal away. Julius wouldn't miss him and if he retired to the library, his cousins would only harangue him about being the next one to wed—a subject he'd had quite enough of for one day.

Quickly, Francis made his way to Lord and Lady Tilney who were speaking to his parents. "Thank you, my lady, my lord. A lovely wedding and wedding breakfast. My brother is the luckiest of men."

"Thank you, Mr. Price." Lady Tilney fluttered a bit until another pair of guests drew her attention away from him. He bowed and turned to his parents. "Mother, Father, I'm off to my club for the evening."

"You're not staying until your brother leaves on his wedding trip, Francis?" His mother had begun to frown.

"Julius and Augusta are cleaning up after a mishap with the

cake. I daresay it will take them some time to put everything to rights. You know how newly married couples are." Francis smiled sweetly at his mother but sent a knowing glance to his father.

"Francis is a grown man, Elizabeth. Let him make his own decisions." Thank God Father was made of sterner stuff. "I'll see you tomorrow at breakfast."

"Thank you, Father." He leaned over and kissed his mother's cheek. "Don't worry, Mother. I promise I will know how to leave on a wedding trip even if I do not witness Julius's departure firsthand."

"Yes, but when will your wedding trip take place, Francis? Or your wedding for that matter. You have not seemed interested in any of the young ladies out this past Season, nor anyone in the Little Season either." His mother fixed him with a stern eye that said she wanted answers and she wanted them now. "Lady Jarius's granddaughter is to come out this Spring. We could call on her in the next week or so." She smoothed out his jacket collar. "Nothing wrong with getting an advance look at the field."

"The Quartermain cousins have suggested Grandfather and Grandmother host a house party in March and invite a bevy of young ladies—and not so young ones also I suspect—for me to look over as well." The whole idea made him feel like he was at Tattersall's looking over cattle to purchase. "Will that suit you, Mother?"

"I'm not certain Mama and Papa are up to hosting a house party." Mother bit her lip, torn between the possibility of assisting her son in winning a wager and her knowledge of her parents' capabilities.

"I'm sure if we offer to help, the duke will be more than willing to host such an event." Father himself seemed excited by the prospect. "Besides, he can always hire more servants if need be. I'll speak to him first thing tomorrow. You know he'll do anything for a wager."

"Even work to lose it if it means getting his way." Francis tried to keep the bitterness out of his voice. His parents had no idea why he was reluctant to marry, but then no one did.

"Papa would cut off his nose to spite this face and sharpen the knife with which he did it if it served his purposes regarding a wager." Mother seemed awfully cheerful about her parent's legendary tenacity.

"Now that I do believe." Francis kissed his mother once more. "But I must go before Tom or one of the others finds me. I will see you at breakfast, Father." Turning to leave, Francis caught a glimpse of Alex, his head sweeping the rooms as if looking for someone. Francis bolted for the foyer, hastily retrieved his hat, coat, and stick and managed to escape out into the chill air of the late afternoon, heaving a sigh of relief as he was swallowed up in the brisk foot traffic heading away from Mayfair.

Starting off quickly down the smooth pavement of the side-walk, his pace slowing a trifle as he lost the feeling that one of his cousins was about to apprehend him and drag him back to the breakfast.

Setting his feet toward the nearby neighborhood of Soho, Francis followed the way he knew so well that wound toward Marleybone, though that was not his final destination. His pace warmed him well against the chill as the sun continued its slide toward the end of the earth. He turned left into Tottenham Court Road, eagerly quickening his pace now as he strode up to number fifteen Rathbone Place and put his key in the door.

Opening it quickly, he doffed his hat and coat, leaving them on the rack, then headed up the staircase with urgent steps. The door to the bedroom had been left ajar in invitation. Silently, he pushed it open, and his breath caught in his throat.

The slender woman sat at the toilet table pushed against a wall, a lamp illuminating her creamy skin, making her seem to glow in the soft light. The stark difference between the pale skin and long raven-black tresses that cascaded down her back in thick waves made his cock spring to life. Absorbed in applying a touch of rouge to her cheeks, she seemed unaware of him and Francis stood quietly, drinking in the sheer beauty that dazzled him every time he entered the chamber. Alabaster skin, ebony hair, eyes of the purest green tilted up slightly at the ends with thick sooty lashes, and high cheekbones that always seemed to bloom like pink roses above her long, slender neck.

Her China-blue-silk robe hid the rest of her, just barely, although he knew every inch of her lovely body intimately. From her perfectly round breasts with the deep, rosy nipples, to her slender waist that tended to be ticklish, to her curvaceous hips, to the dark thicket of curls that called to him so potently this moment he had to shift himself to keep his member from tenting his trousers.

The slight movement caught her attention and she looked up from the mirror, her luscious red lips curling into a welcoming smile. "You are early, my love. I wasn't expecting you until much later."

"My brother decided to dally with his new wife so I thought I would take a page from his copy book and come here to you now." Francis moved to stand behind her, then put his hands on her slim shoulders and bent to kiss the swan-like neck, starting at the warm pulse beneath her jaw, then trailing down until he was impeded by her dressing gown. "I wish you could have been with me at the wedding, Gem."

"You know that wasn't possible, my love." She arched her back and laid her head against his chest.

"It would if you would just agree to marry me." He parted her robe, then turned her around to kiss her breasts.

"Francis, we have talked about this many times." She frowned into the mirror, but her eyes were sad. "A man of your breeding marries a virtuous young lady who has family and position and wealth. He does not marry his mistress."

"I would, if only you would accept me, my love." He would marry her this minute, uncaring what Polite Society or his family might think. But she'd been steadfast in her refusals for the past three years. Sadly, he knew he would not change her mind tonight, so he'd do the next best thing—the only thing she would allow him to do—and show her how much he loved her. "But I have good news for you tonight."

Her smile widened. "We will have the whole night together?"

"Yes." Francis slid his hands down to cup her magnificent breasts, reveling in the feel of them. "I won't have to leave until morning this time."

Graceful as a bird, she rose and turned to face him. "That is the best news possible, my love." She untied her robe and let it slip to the floor, leaving her gloriously naked before him.

He caught his breath, as he always did, at her exquisite beauty, his cock bumping insistently against his trousers, struggling to be free. "You are lovelier each time I behold you, Gem." Cupping her breasts again, he bent to taste first one, then the other, his arousal getting harder by the moment.

"Let me take care of you, love." Gem began to strip his clothes from him all the while he continued to kiss and caress every inch of her he could reach, until finally she plucked his boots and trousers off, so he stood as naked as she was.

"You always do, sweetheart." He tugged her toward the waiting bed, kissing her frantically, unable to wait much longer to sink himself into her velvety heat. He pulled her into the bed, covered her and groaned as his body sought the ultimate pleasure once more with the woman of his dreams.

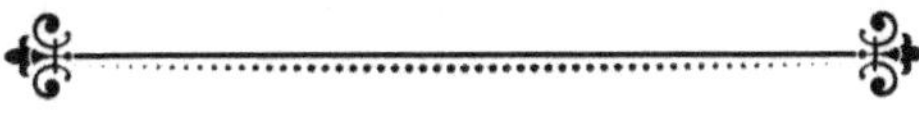

EPILOGUE

Cairo, Egypt
April 1, 1861

A WARM WIND blew in the diverse scents of the city, making Augusta breathe deeply, delighting in the pungent aromas of the Egyptian night. The balcony of their suite in the Shepheard Hotel overlooked the Nile, where all manner of boats plied their way here and there. She spotted a *dahabiya*, a houseboat with sails like the one they had spent more than a month on, sailing from Cairo to Luxor and back. Memories of climbing pyramids, riding camels, exploring tombs with real mummies all flooded her mind, making her smile broadly into the soft night. In the past two months she'd had enough adventures to last a lifetime. Almost.

The suite was high up and faced the broad river, so Augusta could see but not be seen by any prying eyes. And as the balcony wall came up to her chest, she'd taken to wearing only her sheerest robe whenever she stepped onto the balcony, not only to combat the oppressive heat, but to savor the feeling of being daring and adventurous each time she did so.

Life with Julius had been nothing but daring and adventurous these past weeks. True to his word, they had explored all manner of ways to pleasure one another in the first destination of their wedding trip, an apartment in Venice—making good use of the huge, soft bed, of the big leather sofa, and the small kitchen table…Her face heated whenever she recalled the loud clatter of the pots and pans they'd knocked to the floor during that particular session of vigorous amorous congress—and the manager's curious face at the door when he came to check on them.

"Penny for your thoughts." Julius's voice in her ear would have made her jump had she not sensed his presence behind her as soon as he stepped out onto the balcony. Such a thing had become almost another sense—like seeing or hearing—to know instinctively when he had entered a room, whether she could see him or not.

"You always know what I'm thinking about, my love." She arched her back against his naked body as he wrapped his arms around her, filling his hands with her breasts, her core aching immediately at his touch.

"Yes, but which one of our amorous exploits were you think-ing of?" He touched the shell of her ear with his tongue, and she shivered.

"The kitchen of course." Augusta bit back a moan as he ex-pertly tweaked her nipples, bringing them immediately to hard points that throbbed exquisitely.

"One of my favorite memories as well." His lips strayed down her neck and she stretched it to give him greater access. One hand left her breast and suddenly he dragged her filmy robe upward, her derriere cooled by the soft breeze. Spreading her legs apart, Julius pushed his hard, hot member right against her entrance.

Augusta stiffened, her wide eyes taking in the river before her and the street directly below them where people walked, unaware of what was transpiring above them. This was wicked indeed. "Here? On the balcony?" she whispered.

"It's dark. No one can see us." He ran the tip of his tongue down the nape of her neck. "They may hear us, but no one will know where the noises come from, and they won't mind the cries of love on a warm night." His breath was hot in her ear, making her shiver with desire.

"You are a scandalous man, Lord Boxted." She arched her back, pressing herself against him in invitation.

"Because you bring out the wickedness in me, my love." He thrust forward, Augusta thrilling as always at the exquisite feeling of being filled by him. She closed her eyes and moaned softly in contentment.

"Give me your hand."

Curious, but too used to his inventive love play to question him, she took one hand off the wall and put it in his. He drew it forward, leaning into her as he did so until he was seated completely inside her. Augusta gasped, then moaned louder with the pleasure his body always brought her.

"Here." He placed her fingers on her nub.

"What...?" He'd always played there before.

"Do as I have done here. I wish to play with both your nipples, so you must be my hand there tonight."

Startled at the strange idea, she nodded. She'd done many things at Julius's behest in the past months that had yielded so much pleasure, she no longer questioned him at all. Dutifully, she gave the little nub a tentative stroke. Her body gripped his member, flooding her core with the same spiraling sensations his hand did when it played there. She groaned as he began to move within her.

Filling his hands with her breasts once more, his nimble fingers rolled and tweaked her nipples, making them harden and ache in such a good way. She picked up the rhythm he set down below, stroking herself as he thrust in and out. All of these astounding sensations built her excitement so quickly she couldn't control her increasingly loud moans. Spiraling to the ultimate peak with an unexpected quickness, her climax took her by surprise so she screamed his name as her whole body exploded, wave after wave of the most intense pleasure washing through her.

The echo of her cry was followed almost immediately by

Julius calling her name as he strained against her, spilling himself into her as her body continued to clasp and release him.

That pinnacle had lasted longer than any other, at least it seemed that way to Augusta, her legs so weak they wobbled. She clung to the balcony wall as Julius withdrew, then pulled her back into the room, to the big sofa before the fireplace. He gathered her to him, and she curled up beside him, her head lolling against his chest, thoroughly spent and oh, so satisfied.

They remained that way for some minutes, until their breathing slowed and Augusta could collect her thoughts enough to speak. "I believe that has now surpassed the kitchen as the most erotic amorous congress we have had."

Julius grinned down at her, wrapping her in his arms. "I thought it might."

She rubbed her cheek against his warm skin, the salty scent of him wonderfully familiar. If only they could stay like this forever, she would be the most content woman in the world.

"I'm glad we have so many delightful memories of our trip to Venice and Cairo, my love, because I'm afraid we must leave for home."

"But I thought we were to stay until the end of April at least." She'd loved their private life here, away from family and friends, doing exactly as they wished every day. "I'm not ready to give up our idyllic life here, Julius."

"I'm sorry, love, but I've had a letter from Alex begging me to come home." His tone had sobered and she looked up to see a worried frown.

"Why? What is wrong?"

"Francis. Alex says something happened at Grandfather's house party and Francis is beside himself."

"Oh, my dear, how awful." She rubbed her cheek against his chest. "I suppose then we must go. Francis is your brother and he needs you. It's just that," she dropped her hand to his deflated cock and gave it a gentle squeeze, "we shall never be able to do the things we've done here back in England."

He sighed and patted her hand. "I daresay we will find other ways to enjoy our love play, even in England." He wiggled his eyebrows at her, making her giggle. "Even if I have to build us a hunting cabin of our own." Then he sobered again. "But yes, Francis appears to be in dire straits if he's threatening to renege on the wager."

"What?" Augusta sat up, shocked. To renege on such an agreement was anathema—especially to a Quartermain. She'd come to understand that well. "Why?"

"Alex said he couldn't explain it in a letter, but it was imperative we come home immediately as Francis is swearing he will not marry under any circumstances. All the cousins are in an uproar, save Tom, who didn't want to marry anyway. He begs me to return to try to talk some sense into my brother."

Augusta kissed her husband softly on the cheek. "Yes, we must go, my love. Family comes first, I do agree." She cut her gaze sideways at him. "I daresay it will be best to return home now in any case—before the baby makes travel difficult for me."

Julius's head snapped toward her so sharply his neck popped. "What did you say?"

She laughed as his mouth dropped open like a fish gasping for air. "I said we are going to have a baby, Julius. Possibly your heir, although I'd prefer to have a girl first—to insure we will have many more nights of amorous congress like this one, even if they are in England."

"Augusta is it true? Are you sure?"

"I've not been unwell since before Yule's wedding. That may not mean anything, but before then I was unwell so regularly, you could set a clock by me. So I think our tryst in the cabin did the trick." She beamed at him. "If you wish to have many children, my love, I'd say building our own cabin would be an excellent idea."

Julius pulled her to him and kissed her with a passion that took her breath away. "I'll build you anything you want, my love. A cabin, a palace, a home with a balcony overlooking the water like this one. Then we can dismiss all the servants and frolic as we wish whenever we wish." He hugged her to him so fiercely, she thought her ribs would crack. "I love you so much, Augusta. So much I cannot possibly tell you how much I love you."

"I love you too, Julius. More than you know." She laid her head against his chest again, happier and more content than ever in her life. "If you build the house with the balcony, you must promise me one thing."

"Name it, my love."

"Every room must have a chess set." She grinned at him. "I insist on being able to best you in any room of the house."

"Whatever you wish, sweetheart." He chuckled and wrapped his arms more firmly around her. "You have already won my heart, so I have nothing left to lose."

The End

About the Author

Jenna Jaxon is a best-selling author of historical romance, writing in a variety of time periods because she believes that passion is timeless. She has been reading and writing historical romance since she was a teenager. A romantic herself, Jenna has always loved a dark side to the genre, a twist, suspense, a surprise. She tries to incorporate all these elements into her own stories.

She lives in Virginia with her family and a small menagerie of pets—including two vocal cats, one almost silent cat, two curious bunnies, and a Shar-pei mix named Frenchie.

Blog: www.jennajaxon.wordpress.com
Facebook: facebook.com/jenna.jaxon
Twitter: @Jenna_Jaxon
Instagram: passionistimeless
TikTok: @jennajaxon1

www.ingramcontent.com/pod-product-compliance
Lightning Source LLC
Chambersburg PA
CBHW070352310726
48977CB00002B/411